Rescuing Mila

Squadron 6

Claire Boston

I0582941

BANTILLY
PUBLISHING

First published by Bantilly Publishing in 2025

Rescuing Mila: Squadron 6

EPUB format: 9781922916136
Print: 9781922916143
Large Print: 9781922916150

Cover design by EmCat Designs
Edited by Ann Harth
Proofread by Teena Raffa-Mulligan

About the Author

Claire Boston fell in love with romance and romantic suspense at eleven when she discovered her mother's stash of Nora Roberts novels. Like Nora, she writes series set around families or groups of friends with a guaranteed happy ending.

She loves travelling and learning about new cultures and interesting vocations which she then weaves into her writing.

When Claire's not at the computer typing her stories she can be found creating her own handmade journals, swinging on a sidecar, or in the garden attempting to grow something other than weeds.

Claire lives in Western Australia with her husband, who loves even her most annoying quirks and is currently learning how to knit.

You can find her complete book list on her website FAQ page www.claireboston.com/pages/faq

You can connect with Claire through Facebook and TikTok, or join her reader group

(https://www.claireboston.com/pages/reader-group/).

Also by Claire Boston

Chapter 1

Mila Watkin blinked. It couldn't be. She tracked the blonde head of hair weaving above the mass of dark-haired Indonesian locals at the market, hoping her eyes were deceiving her.

They had to be.

No way on earth Vance Bradley would be on a remote Indonesian island without indoor plumbing, paved roads, or any modern conveniences besides a single bar and small medical centre.

It was way beneath him.

Heart pounding, she ducked into a fruit stall, greeted the owner, and peered out into the square.

Stylish beach-blond hair, a too-perfect nose, aqua polo shirt to bring out the blue in his eyes, pressed beige linen slacks and boater shoes.

Yep, it was definitely him.

Her chest tightened, and she exhaled.

What was he doing here?

Though she wanted to believe he'd travelled all this way from Sydney to beg her forgiveness, and profess his undying love, she wasn't delusional.

Not anymore.

Not since she'd caught him in bed with another woman.

Bastard.

"Is something wrong, Mila?" Ibu Minar asked in Indonesian.

Mila jumped and looked down at the older woman who owned the stall. "I'm not sure." As she watched, Pak Agus, the man who controlled the island, joined her ex-fiancé. They smiled and shook hands as if they were best friends. Agus was dressed in a similar style to Vance, which would have appealed to Vance's snobbery.

Money didn't buy you class.

Concern filled her. How on earth did Vance know the smuggler? More than likely, Agus had made it a point to introduce himself when word reached him that a rich white man had arrived on the island.

But if Vance was looking for her, he could have told Agus things about Mila that she'd gone to great lengths to hide from Agus.

She had avoided Agus since she'd gone through the obligatory meeting with him when she'd arrived. He liked to know who was on his island and had questioned her extensively about her background. His far too casual body language had triggered her wariness. Years of her mother picking out those most likely to cause trouble whenever they went out had rubbed off and Mila had kept quiet about the fact her mother was a major-general in the army and her father owned a very successful business back home in Sydney. Instead, she'd played the role of the backpacker trying to find herself.

Which wasn't far from the truth.

"Oh, there is Pak Agus!" Ibu Minar waved and called out, "Pak, please try one of my rambutans."

Mila winced, but it was too late to hide. Agus turned and spotted her. He tapped Vance on the shoulder and pointed.

Damn it.

"Mila!" Vance cried, and several people in the square turned to look. Foreigners weren't common here as Pulau Tengah wasn't set up for tourism. Usually only die-hard surfers ventured all this way looking for the perfect wave.

It was one reason Mila was here—to teach the locals English so they could expand into tourism.

Mila moved out of the stall, not wanting to get stuck in a confined space. "Vance. What are you doing here?"

He grinned that bright smile of his which she'd once thought was charming. "Looking for you, of course." He smiled at Ibu Minar and pulled out a ten dollar note, handing it to her. "I'll have some of those."

Ibu glanced at Agus who translated for her and told her he would convert the note into rupiah for her, and then she pocketed the money and happily bagged the rambutan.

Vance liked to splash money about, but hadn't even taken the time to get the correct currency. His apparent generosity had appealed to her until she'd realised he'd only done it when he'd had an audience.

"Why?" She hadn't had the energy to yell at him when she'd caught him in bed with another woman, but she'd been extremely clear in her breakup text.

He had the grace to look bashful. "I never had the opportunity to apologise. The guilt has been gnawing at me." His sincerity was so convincing Mila took a half step forward before she stopped herself. Vance's earnest smile slid its way around her. "Can we talk at your place?"

She shook her head. This was all an act, though worthy of an Oscar. She couldn't be fooled this time. "No." She wasn't letting him into her little one- room long house. It was her sanctuary and she didn't want any association of him there.

"Why don't we go back to my place for a drink?" Agus suggested, his tone smooth and friendly, but his dark eyes never left her like a snake ready to strike.

Goosebumps leapt on her skin. He knew she'd lied, maybe even knew who her mother was. That was the only reason he'd take time out of his day to help Vance track her down.

Going to his house was an even worse idea, but before she could come up with an excuse, Agus smiled at her, his eyes hard. "I insist."

Damn. Fear gripped her and she glanced around, but there was nowhere to run, nowhere to hide. Her mother and brother, Jared, who had also joined the military, would tell her not to go with him, but she had no choice.

No one refused Agus.

He gestured towards his brand new black four-wheel drive on the edge of the square. One of Agus's bodyguards was with the car, and the other was behind Agus.

Vance seemed oblivious to Agus's implied threat. As the son of Australia's Minister for Defence he would have had security training, but knowing Vance, he hadn't paid attention. "Please, Mila. It's just a chat. There are things we should discuss."

Her eyebrows rose. "Like how long you'd been sleeping with that woman?"

Vance held up his hands, but she caught the flicker of annoyance in his eyes before he was all contrite. "Please."

She didn't have a choice. "I have a class in an hour. I need to be back by then."

"I'll make sure you are," Agus assured her. "I wouldn't like my people going without."

His people. Mila caught herself before she rolled her

eyes. Sure, some people like Ibu Minar saw him as a saviour because he'd built the bar and the little medical centre, but most realised any favours came with a lot of sticky strings attached.

She climbed into the four-wheel drive and Vance got in next to her, with one of Agus's men on her other side. Definitely no escaping.

Her mind whirled. If Agus knew who her mother was, Mila couldn't stay. It would be too dangerous.

She only had herself to blame. If she'd told her parents where she was going, her mother would have warned her.

But no, she'd wanted to be decisive for once and had arranged the trip through one of the women her mother had kept in contact with over the years.

It was only after she'd arrived, she'd discovered her mother had arrested Agus when he'd stolen supplies from the relief effort after a tsunami. His engagement to the chief's daughter had been broken and Agus had vowed vengeance.

No one knew exactly what had happened after Agus got out of gaol, but ten years later, he had arrived at the island and taken over.

He'd told everyone her mother had been the thief, not him, and vowed to pay her back someday.

Which meant Mila needed to leave before Agus decided what he wanted to do to her.

The air-conditioning cooled her whirling mind on the ride from the village to the cliff top where Agus's three-storey house was located. Mila closed her eyes as she tried not to panic.

"You look good," Vance said.

Mila didn't answer. She wore a light summer dress she'd picked up at a market on the mainland before catching a boat here. It was cheap and colourful, and exactly the thing Vance would normally suggest she save for dinner with her parents rather than going out in public where *people* might see her.

He wanted something from her.

Of course he did. Why else would he be here? It had taken a couple of months before she'd admitted to herself the main reason she'd accepted his proposal was because she was sick of being so indecisive. She'd flitted from a commerce course, to working with her father, then trying the army reserves and back to do an arts degree, without anything appealing.

Both her brothers had known exactly what they wanted to do after university—one working for her father, the other going into the military—and Mila felt inadequate, flighty even. People had started looking at her with pity or amusement when they asked where she was working.

So when Vance had proposed, she'd not wanted to appear indecisive in her love life.

The car pulled up in front of Agus's concrete monstrosity.

Aside from the medical centre in town, it was the only building made of concrete, but it had been painted a rich earthy orange similar to a Spanish hacienda. The gardens out the front were beginning to take hold and were full of frangipanis, bougainvilleas, and other lush tropical plants.

Two men with a Belgian Shepherd came around the corner of the house. Security.

Did Agus actually have to worry about his safety, or was this all for show? Mila wasn't certain what illegal activities he took part in, but from the rumours she'd heard, it sounded as if he was part pirate, part smuggler. Maybe he'd made powerful enemies.

As she walked down the path to the front door, she noted another two guards with a dog coming from the other side.

Did he have more covering the back, or didn't they realise how easily someone could scale the cliffs and get in via the back while both guards were at the front?

She hoped the latter, particularly if Agus decided to keep her here.

Inside, the house was cool. Two doors led off the main hallway and stairs led to the next floor. The corridor in front of her led to another door on the opposite side of the house facing the cliffs. She followed Agus and Vance into a lounge room which contained heavy sofas covered in thick brocade, a stupid fabric for this kind of humid climate. Though the air-conditioning was blasting, so perhaps he didn't have to worry about such things as mould.

She shivered as she sat on the sofa Agus indicated. "What do you want, Vance?" The less time she spent here, the better. A strand of her dark hair fell across her face and she quickly undid and redid her loose bun.

"I wanted to apologise." Vance sat next to her and tried to take her hand. She shifted away and clasped both hands in her lap. Agus stood across the room, watching with interest.

"That woman meant nothing to me."

"So you ruined your engagement for nothing?" Was it better that it was just sex? No, neither option made her sympathetic to him.

He pressed his lips together before giving her his sad puppy dog eyes. "She seduced me."

So now it wasn't his fault. God, she'd been so stupid to fall for his charming, loveable rogue act.

Or so desperate to have something in her life that had meaning.

Mila shifted in her seat, wanting to be anywhere but here. She sighed. "Go ahead."

Vance frowned. "What?"

"You said you wanted to apologise," Mila replied. "I

7

haven't heard one yet."

His eyes widened and then he grabbed her hand. "Of course. I'm so sorry I hurt you. Please forgive me."

Mila tried to pull away but Vance held tight. Not wanting to make a scene, she said, "You're forgiven." She'd dodged a bullet finding out about Vance's infidelity before the wedding and it had given her the excuse to break off the engagement so she didn't seem flighty.

Vance sighed in relief. "You're so good to me, Mila. We can return home on the next barge and tell everyone the wedding is still on."

Mila burst out laughing, but Vance stared at her in all seriousness. Her laughter died and her skin crawled. "No."

"But you said you forgave me," Vance said, his expression wounded.

"Yes, because your affair showed me what you're truly like. I'm not marrying you."

Vance's scowl peeled the earnest façade from his face. "My father wants me to settle down, get a proper job, and get married."

The truth hit her and she lost her breath. "That's why you dated me. To get a job with Dad." She acknowledged the hurt even though she didn't care for Vance any longer.

"Right." He agreed as if it wasn't a big deal, shifting into bargaining mode, and her weak heart ached.

She'd been so flattered by his attention and so surprised he'd been interested in her despite the far more glamorous and sophisticated women at the fundraiser.

"We get married, I get my job back at your dad's company and my father continues to pay me my allowance."

Mila switched her attention back to what he was

saying. She stared at him. Was he serious? "And what exactly is in it for me?"

He blinked. "Well, you want to get married, and you can show your face in society again."

She frowned. "I don't understand."

"Well, you must have been embarrassed about the breakup to hide on this backwards island."

He really had no idea who she was. She'd spoken to him about wanting to volunteer in the future, and he mustn't have listened to a word she'd said.

"I'd share some of my money with you."

Some, not all. Out of morbid curiosity, she asked, "How much would you share?"

Vance pursed his lips as if he was making a hard decision. "Ten percent."

A bit of her died inside. Was she worth so little?

Agus shifted to lean against a sideboard, listening to every word. Vance had to stop talking about money. She could practically see the dollar signs in Agus's eyes.

"Firstly, Dad wouldn't reemploy you even if we did marry. You did nothing of value the whole time you worked there."

"Surely he wants to please his little girl."

She shook her head. "I wouldn't ask him to. You're a bad investment." Plus, both her parents had told her how relieved they were that she'd broken off the engagement.

He scowled, the genial bargainer personality glitching for a moment. "I can take you away from this hole, and you can live in my townhouse on Bondi Beach."

"I like this island." Bondi was too crowded for her.

"Be reasonable, Mila. I'm offering you everything you could ever want."

He didn't know what she wanted. Had never cared enough to ask her. "No. You're offering me everything *you* want. We don't want the same things, Vance. We never did."

"You've got to do this, Mila." A hint of desperation now.

"Why? There are plenty of women who would marry you." Plenty who wouldn't look past the shiny sports car and beachfront townhouse.

"I need a job."

She sighed. The only reason he'd sought her out was because of her father. "Then I suggest you apply for one."

"You're so selfish, Mila. I can't believe you won't do this for me."

And here was the child throwing the tantrum. He'd kept this side well-hidden during their relationship.

She was relieved she'd seen the true Vance prior to the wedding, but the fact their entire relationship had been a lie made her sad.

"It sounds as if your father has plenty of money to help one person," Agus said.

Her skin tightened at his curious and slightly menacing tone. She glanced up as Agus approached them.

"I didn't realise your father was so powerful," Agus added.

Mila glared a warning at Vance, but he didn't notice. "My father doesn't have power. He owns a business."

Vance snorted, oblivious to the threat in Agus's words. "A multi-million dollar business."

She slapped his thigh hard, trying to convey *shut the hell up* in her gaze. "It's irrelevant. Agus doesn't need the details."

Agus chuckled. "If I remember correctly, you also said your mother was a team leader at an organisation."

Vance laughed. "Good one, Mila." He turned to Agus. "She's a major-general in the army. That's how we met. Dad's the Minister for Defence and there was some army fundraiser he dragged me to. Mila was there."

Mila wanted to be sick. She took a moment to fantasise about gagging Vance and then stood. "I have to get to my class."

Agus stopped her with a hand on her arm. "Vance has been very forthcoming."

A heavy dread sank to the bottom of her stomach.

Agus smiled. "Did you know I met your mother twenty years ago?"

Mila forced a polite smile to her face. "No, I didn't."

"Yes. Imagine my surprise when Vance told me who she was."

Mila shot Vance a glare. He stared back confused.

"I know what it's like to have marriage plans cancelled. You really should give Vance's proposal proper consideration." His grip tightened on her arm and she winced. "On this island, we believe when you make a big decision, you need to focus all your attention on it. It's better for the soul." He held out his hand. "You need to leave your phone here."

She placed a hand over the bag she always wore crossed over her body. "That won't be necessary."

"Oh, I think it is. And your laptop as well."

She clutched her bag to her chest. If he took both, she couldn't contact anyone back home. "I need my laptop for my classes."

"I'll get Ali to collect it after each class."

Perhaps he wanted to toy with her, or perhaps he hadn't decided what his revenge would be. Or maybe his revenge was making her marry someone she didn't want to marry. She had to leave the island.

Vance smirked. "Good idea. She'll realise my offer is the best thing for her."

Arsehole. "I can think about it while also having my

phone."

"I insist." Agus held out his hand. "Quickly now, or you'll be late for your class."

She would be stuck on the island until Agus changed his mind. No one came or left without Agus knowing.

She understood the threat for what it was. "Yes, Pak." She dug around her bag and her fingers gripped the phone. Slowly she pulled it out and handed it over, noting the strong Wi-Fi signal. So the small bar in the village wasn't the only place to have Wi-Fi—Agus had it here too.

Not that the knowledge helped her if she didn't have a device.

"Vance, might I have a private word before I go?" She glanced at Agus for permission. He inclined his head and smirked. She was trapped, and he was enjoying it.

Quickly she grabbed Vance's hand and dragged him to the door.

"You'll realise marrying me is the best solution," Vance said.

He still had no clue what he'd done. She closed her eyes to channel some patience, because her whole body thrummed with fear. "Do you realise what Agus is, Vance?"

"He's the only decent guy on the island. I was lucky to run into him when I arrived."

Luck had nothing to do with it. "He's a criminal. The reason he's so wealthy is because he's a smuggler. He's dangerous."

Vance's eyes widened. "You've been watching too many movies."

"He took my phone."

"To give you the time to consider my offer."

She glared at him. "Half the villagers are terrified of him. I kept under his radar and now you've told him who I am. What do you think a man like that will do with this information?"

"Chill, Mila. You're blowing things out of proportion."

Imbecile. How could he be so clueless? "If I were you, I'd leave right now, before he forces you to stay too."

Instead of the fear she'd expected, his forehead crumpled in contemplation. She didn't want to know what he was thinking.

"Goodbye, Vance." She'd done her best to help him. What he did from here wasn't her responsibility. She got into the car and Ali drove her back to the village for her class.

Mila stared out the window down to the small village below, her heart aching.

She'd been happy here. It was a safe place to nurture her broken heart and figure out what she wanted out of life.

But she could no longer stay.

Not now Agus knew who she was.

She rubbed the chill from her arms.

She just had to figure out how to leave without Agus stopping her.

Chapter 2

Sergeant Damien "Dobby" Dobson stared out at the blackness of the night, broken only by the glisten of the ocean not far below. The roar of the helicopter rotors was background noise, the usual accompaniment for the start of a mission. What wasn't normal was the way his stomach clenched as the feeling things were about to go FUBAR intensified and they hadn't even arrived at Pulau Tengah.

They shouldn't be here.

There hadn't been nearly enough time to plan for all contingencies.

But the Minister for Defence's son had been kidnapped and Dobby's team had to rescue him before the twenty-four-hour deadline passed, or he would be killed.

By all reports, the party boy often took these kinds of holidays where sampling the local 'wares' was part of the fun, though his father insisted he'd gone to win back his ex-fiancée, who was teaching English there.

Luckily the ex-fiancée was the daughter of a major-general who had immediately been called for more information. She hadn't been able to get in touch with her daughter, as internet was sporadic on the island, though she had told them a man named Agus ran the island.

Her daughter, Mila, believed he was some kind of smuggler or pirate. Probably a small fish in the scheme of things, but smart enough to take advantage of an opportunity when he saw it.

The Major-General also mentioned Agus hated her, but Mila had hidden their relationship from the man.

Vance might have changed that. At least the Major-General hadn't also received a ransom demand.

An inexperienced thug with little fire power wouldn't be hard to overcome, but he also might have enough fire power to lack sense.

They hadn't been able to source blueprints of the man's house and had not much more than some satellite imagery of the island and a rough location of where the ex lived in the main village of Batara.

None of that mattered to the minister and his wife. The high priority mission had been planned and green-lit in less than five hours and because Dobby's team was in the area taking part in an international war game, they'd been ordered to go.

He considered it lucky they'd at least received photos of Vance and his ex, Mila, although by all accounts, few tourists went to the island.

The Major-General wanted an update on her daughter's whereabouts if possible, which Dobby considered a reasonable request. He'd make sure the woman was safe, because she might be next on the smuggler's radar.

Only five minutes to the drop zone.

He checked his team.

Joker sat staring at the floor, mentally preparing himself as he did every mission. His dark hair was still short from their last mission in the Middle East where he'd gone undercover. His Middle Eastern heritage and ability to speak Farsi made him the perfect person, but the mission had been difficult.

Next to him was Hawk. Just under six feet tall and stocky, his dark brown hair was shaggy, and he was a tank.

"Two minutes." Radar's voice was loud in the headset and Dobby turned to their signal operator.

His black hair was tied back in a bun and his broad shoulders touched the side of the chopper and Axle who was next to him. Calm blue eyes watched Dobby, who gave him a nod of acknowledgement. Radar's slight smile was hard to discern beneath his bushy beard.

"Yippee ki-yay," Axle responded, a hint of sarcasm in his tone, his beach- blond hair hidden under his helmet.

Yeah, none of them were thrilled with the way the mission had been planned, but they'd deal with it together.

While Dobby's gut told him this mission was going to suck, he knew his team would have his back.

Pity they were one man down, with Duke injuring himself yesterday.

The little voice in his head which had questioned whether it was time to get out of the army grew in volume. He blocked it out.

He still loved what he did, the challenges and making a difference in the world, but the restrictions were beginning to strangle him. He wanted complete control.

"One minute out," the pilot said over the comms.

The team readied themselves. They were flying under the radar because there hadn't been time to negotiate with the Indonesian government—something else that could put them in hot water on this already rushed mission.

The drop zone was just beyond the horizon from the island. Most of the land was mountainous, so people arrived by boat as there wasn't an airstrip.

They should have two Zodiacs for built-in redundancy, but because of the distance of the ship from the drop zone, they'd had to keep equipment to a minimum to get a better range for the helicopter. Command thought they'd be in and out and wouldn't need a lot.

Dobby knew from experience it was better to plan for the worst.

At least they'd identified the house most likely owned by Agus, due to its size and position on the cliff overlooking the ocean.

But that's all they had.

Dobby sighed.

They reached the drop zone and the Zodiac hit the water followed by Joker and the rest of the team.

Dobby hit the warm water and surfaced, giving the OK to the men in the helicopter and then checking his pack. The down draught from the rotors spat water at him, making it difficult to see where the raft and his men were. He swam forward as the chopper flew away and as soon as it did, it was easier to make out shapes in the dark water. By the time he reached the boat, the rest of his men were onboard, and he hauled himself up.

Joker had the boat heading for the shore the second Dobby's feet left the water. Their infiltration point was on the north side of the island, one bay around from the main village.

When they landed, they'd trek a couple of kilometres through jungle to reach Batara.

Dobby grimaced. He hated working in the jungle; the humidity, the dense undergrowth, the mosquitoes, and to top it off he was soaking wet. Give him a dry desert any day.

As they reached a small uninhabited islet near the larger island, Joker cut the engine and they rowed the rest of the way to the shore.

The jungle loomed, dark and impenetrable.

And silent.

Where were the bird calls and the insects chirping?

His gut clenched as he scanned the area with his night vision goggles. They carried the zod to the back of the beach and tied it to a tree before covering it in leaf litter, removing all sign. Thankfully it was high tide and they didn't have to carry it far. If all went to plan, they'd be back in less than two hours, and it was unlikely any villagers would wander the jungle at this time of night.

Dobby checked his men and adjusted his goggles, taking a step forward only to have the ground tremble beneath him. His heart pounded as he searched for the source.

Nothing but darkness.

"Earthquake," Joker called.

The rumbling increased, and the trees shook, leaves and branches falling around them.

Dobby struggled to stay upright and swore. "Back to shore."

He heard faint cries from the village in the distance.

The shaking continued as Dobby reached the shore and spaced his feet to better balance. The roar was disconcertingly loud and trees leaned and bent with the shaking. A couple of loud cracks further in the forest followed by crashes proved not all the trees had been able to withstand the force.

At this rate, it would be lucky if half the houses in the town remained standing.

"Abort?" Joker asked.

Dobby shook his head. His orders were clear. Don't

come back without the hostage.

But an earthquake of this magnitude meant people would be outside, assessing damage, looking for survivors, instead of being tucked up in bed asleep.

They would stand out when they went looking for Mila.

The FUBAR premonition in his stomach intensified.

For all they knew, the hostage could have been crushed by debris, or roads they'd identified to get them in and out of the village could be blocked.

This was going to be a clusterfuck.

The trembling subsided. "Let's move," he said. "We'll reassess when we get to the village."

He headed into the jungle, prepared for the worst.

***

Mila had given up trying to sleep sometime around midnight. She couldn't stop worrying about how to get off the island.

After class, Ali had taken her laptop and though Mila had asked around, no one had a phone or computer she could use.

In desperation she'd packed her things and headed for the jetty to catch the evening barge to the neighbouring island which had a small airstrip. She hated leaving without saying goodbye, but her gut was screaming at her that it wasn't safe to stay.

The apologetic captain had said there was no room, when the deck was clearly empty.

That's when Ali had wandered towards her and reminded her she couldn't leave until she'd thought about Vance's proposal.

In other words, she wasn't leaving until Agus said so.

Mila had returned to her long house to regroup and spotted one of Agus's other men lounging across the market square watching her.

Which meant there was no point taking her moped and riding to the other coastal villages in the hope of finding someone who would take her to the neighbouring island.

Agus had loyal men in each village and radios with which to contact them since there weren't reliable telecommunications on the island.

No one would let her leave.

Mila's options boiled down to swimming to the nearest habitable island, which was about three kilometres away, and hoping Agus hadn't told anyone to be on the lookout for her, or stealing a boat in the middle of the night and hoping she'd have enough fuel to get her to mainland Sumatra.

So drown, or get stranded in the middle of the ocean, while also stealing someone's livelihood.

She'd considered packing the essentials and a lot of food and hiding in the jungle until Agus had forgotten about her, but she doubted he would forget. The moment she reappeared she'd be in exactly the same dilemma as she was now.

Unable to come up with another option she allowed herself time to fantasise about the dozen ways she would deal with Vance the next time she saw him, the most satisfying of which would be breaking his nose.

Sure, he'd pay for the best plastic surgeon to fix it, but his vanity would take a real kick and he'd lock himself indoors for the time it took to heal, not wanting anyone to see him as anything other than perfect.

In one conversation, Vance had destroyed her anonymity. Mila had stayed off Agus's radar for three months. As far as he was concerned, she was a bleeding heart white woman who was finding herself by teaching English to the villagers.

Now, thanks to stupid Vance Bradley, she was in a

real mess.

Her bed trembled, and she clenched her muscles to stop shaking.

A low roar filled her ears and then the frantic shouts in Indonesian pushed her up on her elbows. She wasn't shaking, the ground was.

Earthquake.

Shit.

She leapt out of bed and threw on some shorts. What the hell was she supposed to do? Hide under the bed? Stand in the doorway? Run outside?

She stumbled to the window in time to see the long house next to her collapse. People screamed.

Fear gripped her heart.

The walls of her tiny room bowed, and she grabbed her bag, scooped up her sneakers and staggered out of the house as wood shattered behind her.

Bursting from the building, she sucked in a breath of the warm night air. Houses shook around her and the ground roared like a jet engine coming in to land. People stumbled into the streets looking as if they were drunk, and moved towards the clear market square.

Right. Get away from the buildings which could collapse. Mila threw her bag strap over her head and followed the others, struggling to stay upright. The ground felt like a carnival ride gone rogue, shifting and shaking, making it impossible to walk in a straight line.

When she reached the group, she slid her sneakers onto her feet and took a breath.

She had twenty children in her English classes, but she couldn't make out faces in the darkness.

The streetlights went out as the shaking subsided, but the noises didn't. Frantic shouts, screams for help, and the scratch and crash of items which hadn't been able to withstand the force of the quake. Mila slowly turned, taking it all in. The front awning of her own building had collapsed, blocking the entrance and exit, and so many other structures were teetering or piles of rubble.

Where was Vance? She glanced up to the cliff which overlooked the village. From here it appeared as if the house still stood. He should be fine.

What did she do now?

"Miss, miss." Someone tugged on her hand and she blinked away the shock to look down at one of her students, Dewi.

"My *nenek* is trapped. She can't get out."

Mila squeezed the ten-year-old's hand. "Show me where."

The scope of the damage became clear as people found torches or lanterns and switched them on. Nearby, a power line was sparking, dangling across the road. Streets were buckled and so many buildings had simply collapsed.

She followed Dewi to a building on the opposite side of the square. Dewi was one of five children, but she lived with her extended family, which included aunts, uncles, cousins and her grandmother, who was trapped.

"This way." Dewi went to climb through a gap in the wall and Mila stopped her.

"It might not be safe."

Dewi frowned at her and shook off her hand. "She's through here."

Before Mila could say anything else, Dewi had slipped through the gap. Fear gripped Mila, but everyone was busy digging through the rubble or searching for family members. She had to be brave. Hopefully the rest of Dewi's family was somewhere safe.

Taking a deep breath, she followed the child into the kitchen. Two outside walls had fallen inward to form a tee-pee space, but any further aftershocks might cause them to collapse.

Mila sniffed, screwing up her nose at the gas smell. Probably from a broken pipe, but she checked the little cooker to make sure everything was off.

Dewi waited impatiently in the doorway. "This way."

"Where's the rest of your family?" Mila asked as she followed the girl.

"They went to visit my uncle in the mountains. He is getting married, but Nenek was too frail, so I stayed with her."

At least there were fewer people to worry about here, but the mountain village would have been hit by the earthquake too. She reached into her bag for her phone and remembered it had been stolen. No torch.

A groan to her left made her turn.

Dewi's grandmother lay underneath a section of the wooden ceiling which had collapsed. Mila hurried over. "Ma'am, are you hurt?" she asked in Indonesian.

"My arm is broken."

OK. Not too bad. At least she could walk. "We'll get you out of here." She examined the chunk of woven ceiling. It didn't appear to be holding anything else up. If she and Dewi could lift it, Dewi's grandmother could get out.

Dewi had already cleared the debris away from the ceiling section and was waiting for instruction.

"Take that side." Mila pointed to the far side, which should be slightly lighter for the child. "On the count of three, we'll lift and move it to the side."

Dewi nodded as Mila shifted into position.

"One, two, three." She hefted the ceiling, grunting at its weight.

Dewi's grandmother groaned and Dewi dropped her section of the ceiling and dashed to her side.

Mila strained as the full weight of the ceiling panel

fell to her and she shoved it against the wall. By the time she turned, Nenek was standing and Dewi was helping her to the exit.

The gas stench was getting stronger.

"Is there a gas valve anywhere?" she asked Nenek as she joined them.

"Outside against the wall."

Mila scanned the kitchen for a splint for Nenek's arm and grabbed a couple of towels on her way out. "Take her into the square," she told Dewi. "I'll join you in a second."

She made her way around the house and located the two gas bottles. One hose had been disconnected, so she turned the tap off. As she was heading back to the square, the first aftershock hit.

She swayed as the ground trembled, her heart racing and people shouting. Crashes came from all around her and she stumbled towards the square. Something brushed her back as she rounded the house but she didn't stop to see what was collapsing behind her. She didn't stop until she reached Dewi and her grandmother.

By then the trembling had stopped.

She exhaled, breathing deeply as her heart rate came down. "Let me check your arm." Mila gently examined Nenek's bruised arm. The bone hadn't broken through the skin, but there was an unnatural bend to it. The nearest medical centre was a street back from the ocean. It was likely to be inundated by people already, but Mila couldn't help her. "I'll take you to the doctor."

Nenek shook her head. "No. *Desa Agung*."

The nearest village was a twenty-minute drive away in the mountains. They were likely to have been hit by the earthquake as well. "The medical centre is closer."

"No," Nenek insisted. "Tsunami."

Mila froze. The air swooshed out of her lungs as she

scanned the area. Those who had found their loved ones were climbing onto scooters and heading east up the mountain. Only those who were searching for missing people stayed.

She should have thought of it. The earthquake and subsequent tsunami twenty years ago was why Mila's mother had visited the island. And her mother's memories of the place had drawn Mila here.

Back then, almost half the population of the island had died because there had been no tsunami early warning systems.

It was clear people knew exactly what to do this time.

Mila nodded and asked, "Do you have a vehicle?"

The grandmother yelled to a nearby woman and in moments they had arranged transport in an already overloaded truck.

"Come," the grandmother demanded.

Mila had her own scooter, and she wouldn't fit inside the truck.

"Miss Mila!" The scream made her spin around. Another one of her students, Fajar, ran towards her, eyes wide, and tears streaming down his face.

"What is it?"

"I can't find my family."

She glanced at Dewi and Nenek and then towards the ocean. Though every instinct told her to run, she couldn't leave this child alone. She waved them away and turned her attention to the boy. "Where were you when the earthquake struck?"

He pointed, and she ran to the neighbouring building with him.

Hopefully they could find them in time.

Chapter 3

By the time Dobby and his team reached the village, another aftershock had hit and people were streaming up the road towards the mountain. He crouched low behind a tree and frowned. Why was everyone leaving? There would be damage all over the island, and potential landslides the higher they went.

His eyes widened as comprehension hit him and then he swore ripely under his breath.

"What is it?" Hawk asked.

"Radar, get on the comms and find out if we should expect a tsunami." Depending on where the epicentre of the quake was, they may have hours or minutes.

Radar took a knee to set up the long-range equipment while Dobby scanned the people leaving the village.

From his intel, Vance's ex had a place nearby, but she was likely part of the exodus heading into the hills.

"They're estimating an hour," Radar said.

Could they get in, rescue Vance and get back to the zod before the tsunami hit? Maybe.

"Do we need to move the zod?" Joker asked.

Should he split his team? They were already down a

team member and they might have to separate to search for Vance if he wasn't in the house on the cliff. "It's tied in place." Finding Vance and getting him to safety was the priority. They'd work out how to get off the island afterwards.

The road out of town was empty, and he gestured for the team to move across and into the jungle at the edge of the settlement.

His gut clenched. Was he making the right decision? Normally they would have planned for all contingencies, but there hadn't been time.

He focused on the mission. The village had very few people left in it. Few people to notice them sneak in.

But the way this mission was going, someone loyal to the kidnapper would spot them and know exactly who they were.

"Axle and Radar, procure transport," Dobby said. They would need to move fast when they got Vance in order to avoid the tsunami. "Joker, stay here and monitor those leaving town. Maybe you'll get lucky and spot Vance and his kidnappers fleeing, or the ex-fiancée." He scanned the area. "Get the drone up and find out how bad the damage in town is and what roads we can use. Hawk, you and I will search for the woman."

His men nodded and got to work. With Hawk by his side, Dobby slipped from the jungle to the nearest building and worked his way into town.

Chaos. So many buildings had collapsed and people were frantically searching for loved ones. A child, no more than three or four, stood by the remains of a house crying with dirt streaked across her face.

Hawk tapped him on the shoulder and pointed towards the square where a petite white woman was frantically shifting debris from a house while a young boy stood next to her. The woman wore pyjama shorts, a pale tank top and sneakers, with her dark hair tied back in a ponytail. She should be leaving, not lifting things which were too heavy for her.

He picked up the child, unable to just leave her there, and her arms wrapped around his neck. His heart clenched as he moved closer to the ex, and she turned to say something to the boy. Dobby saw her face and his breath caught.

The photo hadn't done her any justice. Fierce beauty.

Determination in her eyes. Stunning.

Mila Watkins. English teacher, the Major-General's daughter, and Vance's ex.

He nodded to Hawk and together they approached, keeping to the shadows of the buildings.

"Fajar, it's too heavy," she said. "We need more help."

"*Jangan pergi*," a voice cried from under the rubble.

Mila answered in rapid Indonesian.

He assessed the situation. Someone was trapped behind the debris which might be blocking a door.

"We helping?" Hawk murmured.

"Yeah."

They strode over. "Where do you need us?" he asked Mila, handing her the child.

She started, her eyes wide as she quickly scanned him, taking in his dark fatigues. Questions crossed her face, but she said, "If we can move this panel, it should leave enough space for Fajar's family to get out."

He nodded and took the opposite side from Hawk. Together they shifted the heavy panel away from the house. Before they had even put it down, people were crawling out of the space. He and Hawk crouched behind the panel. The fewer people who saw them the better. A woman swept the small boy into her arms, while a man spoke rapidly to Mila. She handed him the child and the man tugged Mila, gesturing to the mountain.

Mila responded, pointing to a moped across the square and the father herded his family away. Mila turned her attention to them. "What are Australian Special Forces doing here?"

He suppressed a smile at her no-nonsense tone. "Mila Watkins?"

She nodded once, her expression wary. "Did my mother send you?"

He shook his head. "We were hoping you might know who kidnapped Vance Bradley."

"Vance has been kidnapped?" She frowned. "When? I saw him... yesterday."

Dobby scowled. "What time?"

"Midday. He turned up unexpectedly." Her laugh was full of derision. "Now Agus knows who I am. He took my phone and laptop so I couldn't contact anyone."

This wasn't making any sense. "Vance was with Agus—the smuggler?"

She nodded. "I think he's staying with him."

Dobby swore. "We thought Agus was the one who'd kidnapped him. Is there anyone else here who could have done it? Did Vance seem worried about anything?"

She pursed her plump lips. "It's possible that with all of Vance's bragging about money, Agus decided to seize the opportunity." She hurried down the street towards a sobbing woman trying to clear debris from her house.

Dobby and Hawk followed her, but the man they'd rescued reached the sobbing woman first and he and his wife helped her lift the roof. She darted inside and brought out a crying baby.

Dobby grabbed Mila's hand to stop her moving.

"His parents were sent a ransom video. Showed Vance tied and gagged to a chair in a bedroom."

Mila's frowned deepened. "What kind of room? Do you have a copy of the video?"

Dobby shook his head. "Nice room, pale walls, four-poster queen-sized bed."

"Only place around here with rooms like that is Agus's place."

"You went there yesterday?" Hawk asked.

"Yeah. Vance was fine." She scanned the area. "He was sharing far too much information with Agus. I told Vance Agus was dangerous, but he laughed at me."

Dobby glanced towards the ocean but couldn't see it from here. "How high is the cliff Agus's house is on?"

"About ten metres."

Hawk turned to him. "Would the tsunami miss them?"

A good question and one he didn't have an answer for. "Does Agus have much security?"

"I noticed four men with guns and two Belgian shepherds, but I didn't notice any cameras."

Impressive. Not everyone would notice.

"What about the layout of the house?" Hawk asked.

"I didn't see much. They took me through the front entrance and into a lounge room on the right where I spoke with Agus and Vance. There was another door to the left and stairs leading to the next level. Straight ahead was another door outside to the back of the property."

Dobby appreciated she understood what information to provide. "How many storeys?"

"Three."

"Thank you." He turned to Hawk. "Let's check if the others have found transport." Not that the roads were necessarily clear. Hopefully Joker could tell them. "You need to come with us," Dobby said to Mila.

"We'll get you off the island."

He couldn't leave her here when she could be in danger, not only because of Agus but also the tsunami.

"I can't yet. I need to make sure everyone is out."

"You've done your bit. You need to come now. The tsunami will hit in less than an hour."

She nodded. "Where's the extraction point? I'll meet you there. I have a moped." She pointed to the bike not far away.

No. Splitting up would not go well. "We have to wing it with the tsunami."

She hesitated. "Someone might need me."

"They'll need a lot more help than you can give. We'll get you safe and you can come back with the relief effort." She wasn't his responsibility, but it was more difficult than he'd like to walk away.

"Where's the rendezvous?"

She could be involved with Agus... but his gut told him she wasn't. "If we beat the tsunami, you need to be at the intersection to the road up to the mountains. If we're not there, head up the road until you're safe. We'll find you."

"I'll be there." She hurried towards some shouts in the distance.

"Impressive," Hawk said as they jogged back to where Joker waited.

"Yeah." He glanced back as she disappeared around some rubble.

They moved around the building and found Axle and Radar returning. "There are no vehicles in the village," Axle said. "A couple of mopeds, but not enough."

Shit. "Maybe Agus has one."

"Did you find the ex?" Radar asked.

"Yeah. Target should be in the house on the cliff if they haven't evacuated." They moved into the jungle where Joker waited.

"Any eyes on the target?" Dobby asked.

Joker nodded. "He's in the clifftop house."

"How—"

Joker gestured him over. "I used the drone to scope the house on the cliff. There are three locals in an office on the ground floor arguing and Vance is on the third floor pacing the bedroom."

Pacing? He should be tied up at least. "Any other people in the house?"

"Not that I can see. A car took people to a luxury yacht tied to the jetty. Looked like women and children. I didn't see any men. The captain took it out to sea."

If they made it to deep water they would be safe from the tsunami. Smart. So why hadn't Agus taken Vance?

Maybe he wasn't sure they'd make it.

"They've lost power," Joker added.

"Generator?" Radar asked.

"Doesn't look like it," Joker replied. The drone hovered in front of a top-floor window but at a distance so no one would hear.

Vance used his phone for light and paced the room, occasionally checking the door handle which was locked.

Dobby frowned. "He's got a phone."

"We've got his number," Radar said. "Do we call?"

"No. Let's get in and grab him." Something about the whole situation didn't add up. "Give me a look at the rest of the house."

Joker panned around and Dobby noted doors on every side, but the guards didn't move along the cliff-facing side when they patrolled. "That door."

Hawk nodded. "It'll give us more time. We can leave via the front on the way out if we need to."

"You can search for more stairs inside while we get

the target," Dobby told him.

Hopefully they'd find some so they didn't have to go right past the occupied room with Vance who might not be stealthy.

"Only two sets of guards, each with a dog," Joker added.

"There's a four-wheel drive out front," Axle said. "I'll commandeer it."

Good. Finally a plan that would work.

He fished some jerky out of his pack and tucked it into a pocket in case the dogs noticed them and weren't well trained.

They jogged along the edge of the village and up the road to the house, using the darkness to their advantage. The buildings on this side of the village hadn't been damaged by the earthquake. The area they moved through was silent, everyone having long since fled for the mountains.

"We've got thirty minutes tops," Radar murmured when they arrived outside the mansion.

Axle dug around in his pack. "Give me a couple of minutes and I'll have the car ready to go."

Wheels would be a game changer right now.

"Looks like security are at the front," Radar said. "Nothing around the back, Joker?"

Dobby peered around the car. Two sets of guards, each with a Belgian Malinois. The dogs looked half-starved. Agus probably thought hungry dogs made better guard dogs. Idiot.

"No."

That was a massive oversight. Agus didn't know much about good security.

"Joker, stay with Axle," he murmured. "Be our eyes on the ocean and the guards." He gestured to the others to move out.

Dobby ran across the ground, sticking close to the

jungle as they reached the corner of the house. The guards had met in the middle and were conversing.

Good.

His heart pounded in a steady beat as they moved down the wall and along the back of the house.

He tried the door handle and found it unlocked. Finally, something easy. He gestured, and they went through the door, taking up defensive positions.

No alarms.

They crept towards the stairs. Some discussion was happening in the room to the right, but Dobby didn't understand it.

At the top of the carpeted stairs he gestured for Hawk to search for another staircase and he and Radar took the next set of stairs to the third storey.

Dobby counted doors until he got to the one where Vance should be. He tried the handle. Locked.

Radar stood guard while Dobby quickly picked the lock. While it was tempting to smash it open, he'd been commanded to keep it stealthy if he could. Leave no evidence they'd been there, lest they start an international incident.

The lock snicked open and he got to his feet, gesturing to Radar that he was ready.

"Servant stairs to the south," Hawk murmured through the ear comms. "Side exit. Second floor is clear."

Radar nodded to show he'd heard.

Dobby used his fingers to count down and then opened the door, charging into the room, straight to Vance. The man whirled, eyes widened, mouth opened to shout when Dobby clapped a hand over it. "We're getting you out of here, do you understand?" he whispered.

Vance nodded.

"Say nothing and stay between us. You speak, and

you'll give away our position, do you understand?"

Another nod.

Dobby took his hand away. Radar stood guard by the door and Dobby pushed Vance towards him. "Move."

He kept a hand on Vance's shoulder to steady and steer him as he wouldn't have as good sight without night vision goggles.

They jogged down the stairs to the second floor where they met Hawk.

"Guards are heading inside," Joker reported. "Via front door and south side."

Shit. Both doors they'd identified. "Check the ocean," Dobby whispered as they moved out of the stairwell and waited.

Below them were the sounds of men walking past. Hopefully going to report to Agus.

"Water's receding," Joker reported.

Shit. Would the cliff be high enough to miss the brunt of the tsunami? If so, it might be safer to wait here and escape after the first wave hit.

But Agus might fetch Vance to watch the spectacle.

He gestured for them to continue down the stairs. It was doubtful the guards would hear them, but the dogs might.

Radar and Hawk faced opposite directions at the bottom of the stairs and Dobby pushed Vance towards Hawk and the side door. Hawk opened the door as the tsunami warning sirens wailed.

Dobby hoped Mila had left the village.

Vance swore, stumbling to the side, and bumped into something that crashed to the ground.

Voices raised down the corridor.

Shit. Dobby pushed Vance out of the door and Hawk grabbed him. "This way."

Dobby covered the corridor as Radar sprinted out

the door and then closed the door and ran after his team.

"Wave's coming," Joker reported.

They were out of time.

Vance turned towards the ocean, obviously debating whether it was safer inside, but Radar grabbed him and dragged him towards the car. "Move!"

"Axle, how's the car coming?" Dobby called.

"Almost there."

He heard a shout from inside the house and footsteps pounding towards him.

"We've got trouble." He readied a flash grenade and ran after his teammates.

The door opened behind him and he threw the grenade towards it, closing his eyes. "Flash grenade." The others would protect their eyes.

Radar, Hawk and Vance sprinted through the garden. The flash came and went along with a bunch of confused cries.

Gunshots rang out and dirt spat up around him.

He fired back as he turned the corner and raced to the car.

Joker grabbed Vance as they made it to the car. "Get in."

Radar and Hawk took positions on either side of the vehicle as Joker got into the passenger side.

Dobby checked the house and spotted lights moving towards the front door. He pushed harder. "Get in," he called.

Dogs barked from inside and the front door flung wide.

Radar jumped into the backseat, but Hawk took position at the rear, ready to cover Dobby.

It would be a squeeze to get them all inside.

The engine roared to life.

Good work, Axle.

As the dogs raced out of the house, Dobby fished the jerky from his vest. He whistled, getting their attention, and threw it towards them.

The dogs slowed, sniffing.

Hawk leapt on the rear bumper of the four-wheel drive and opened fire as guards burst out of the house.

Dobby added cover fire, splitting their attention before he reached the car and jumped in.

"Go!" Hawk yelled.

Axle gunned it as Radar lay down cover fire out of the car window. Hawk clung to the roof rack as they sped down the hill.

When they were clear, Joker grabbed the drone controller. "Wave's coming in fast."

Hopefully the buildings would slow it down.

Axle slowed as he went around the corner of the village, the jungle to their right, buildings to their left.

Dobby checked on Hawk. He seemed stable on the back of the car and they didn't have time to stop to let him in.

"Where to?" Axle asked.

"The road up to the mountain." They weren't making it back to the boat. All he could hope was the boat survived and would be stuck somewhere in the trees when they searched for it.

As they raced down the road, Dobby saw the wave coming through the buildings, pushing debris in front of it. "Faster!"

"I go much faster and I'll lose Hawk off the back," Axle yelled.

Dobby glanced at the rear of the car. This model had two doors that swung out to access the rear. Maybe they could get one open and Hawk could climb in.

Dobby shifted. "Bend down," he told Vance, shoving his back forward to show what he meant.

"Watch it." Vance tried to resist and Dobby snarled,

"I need to get in the back."

He didn't wait for a reply, just climbed over the seat, kicking Vance in the back as he did so.

"Hawk, move to the side," Dobby called.

Hawk moved and Dobby shoved the lever down, opening one side of the door. The gap was too small for the broad-shouldered man to squeeze through but before Dobby could speak, Hawk was already shifting to the other side so he could open it.

The second door opened with a thud and swung shut again, but Hawk shifted his body to block it. He reached one hand inside and Dobby grabbed it, bracing his legs on the sides of the car. "I've got you."

"Corner!" Axle yelled.

"Hold on!" he yelled to Hawk.

The car rounded the corner. The wave was on the far side of the square where he'd spoken to Mila.

Who was running towards them, the moped nowhere in sight. Fuck. What the hell was she doing there? "Mila!"

Before he processed that, Hawk's foot slipped from the back of the car. "Ah!" His other arm flailed for purchase.

Dobby's arm jolted as Hawk's full weight bore down on him. Radar lunged from the back seat to help, but he was too late.

Hawk's hand slipped from Dobby's grasp and he fell, hitting the ground hard and rolling.

"Stop!" he yelled.

"There's no time," Axle shouted.

Hawk struggled to his feet and turned towards Mila and the wave.

Dobby watched in horror as the wall of water picked up Mila and then Hawk, and swallowed them both.

***

Mila glanced around the square. Everyone was gone, and she took a moment to check whether she could salvage anything from her little room, but she couldn't lift the rubble in front of the door.

As she headed for her moped, she heard a moan. *"Tolong."*

She spun, searching the night for the woman. *"Di mana?"* she called.

A high-pitched, ear-splitting, wailing siren made Mila jump. Definitely time to get out of here. She hesitated and strained to hear over the noise.

"Di sini."

She followed the cry and found Ibu Minar underneath a section of wall next to Mila's room. The old woman was disoriented and had perhaps been knocked unconscious.

Mila tried to block the incessant scream of the siren but glanced towards the ocean. Nothing yet. She hefted the slab of the wooden wall, wishing the two special forces guys would miraculously materialise again and help her.

They didn't, and the slab didn't shift.

Spotting a wooden pole, she dragged it out and used it as a lever to move the panel. It lifted enough for the old woman to shift from under it.

Muscles burning, Mila ensured the woman was clear before she dropped the panel. She panted as she helped Ibu Minar to her feet. The woman screamed in agony. Her foot protruded at an odd angle.

Fighting the urge to vomit, Mila placed her shoulder under the small woman's arm and half lifted her to the moped.

Above the sirens came a low roar that increased in volume.

Shit.

She placed the woman on the bike, stuck the key in

the ignition and turned.

Nothing.

She tried again and again.

The woman pointed at a wire sticking out. "It's come out."

Mila would bet Agus had done it to stop her leaving.

"Wait!" The desperate cry of a child made Mila turn.

The old woman tugged on her arm. "I fix. You go!"

Mila scanned the darkness and spotted a small child who was maybe five hobbling towards them. She left the woman on the bike and ran over. "*Cepat-cepat.*"

She lifted the child into her arms as the moped roared to life. Mila spun to find the old woman at the handlebars, looking over her shoulder. Mila followed her gaze. A black wave bore down on them.

She sprinted to the bike as the old woman accelerated. "Wait!" She shoved the child on the seat behind the woman, but before Mila could get on behind her, the woman took off.

Leaving Mila behind.

Fuck.

She spun. The wave kept coming, moving houses along with it in a wall of debris, mud and foam, far faster than Mila had anticipated. Fear jump-started her heart in a frenetic beat and she sprinted after the moped which was almost out of sight.

The roar of the water increased until she heard nothing else. The ground sloped upwards and her thighs burned as she reached the edge of town. At the intersection ahead of her a black four-wheel drive peeled around the corner, full of black-clothed men, one of whom was hanging on the back.

Suddenly the man on the back fell, landing hard against the road.

The car didn't stop.

The man rolled to his feet and glanced back at her.

"Run!" she screamed.

The water pushed at Mila's feet, overtaking her, and the force of it swept her off her feet and she fell as the swirling surge of sludge surrounded her.

She sucked in a breath before she was dragged under. The power was immense. She felt like a leaf in rapids as she was battered on every side by unseen debris. She tumbled over and over losing track of which way was up.

Her lungs burned and suddenly the water forced her mouth open and she swallowed the muddy, salty liquid.

Mila's stomach revolted, and she gagged, desperately clawing her way to the surface. Her feet hit something hard, and she pushed off it. Finally air touched her face, and she choked in a breath, struggling to stay above the water.

Palm trees flashed by her as the wave hit the jungle and the screech and swoosh of breaking trunks added to the cacophony.

By some act of fate, she was being pushed up the road.

Something grabbed her arm, and she turned to find the soldier right next to her, clinging to a door.

Their eyes met. Rather than fear, she saw determination.

It gave her hope. She grabbed onto the door to stay afloat though the water dragged at her body.

He yelled something, but she caught only a few words. "Turn soon.... grab tree."

Of course. The wave would reach its peak and then turn. If she wasn't careful, it would drag her out with it.

The wave shifted, pushing them towards the jungle. A tree came out of nowhere and they hit it hard, the soldier's hands sliding off the door as he was pulled under the water.

No!

41

She reached for him, but it was no use. He was gone. Then the water ripped the door from her grasp and she fought the pull, her arms burning with the effort to keep her head above the water.

She was almost two kilometres from the shore. Surely the wave had to stop soon.

Tears filled her eyes as her arms grew heavy. One shoe ripped from her foot and her bag pulled against her neck almost choking her.

The water spun her around, and the tempo changed, slowing. She was surrounded by water and debris, but her feet brushed the ground.

The wave had reached its zenith, which meant it would soon start receding, dragging everything with it out into the ocean.

Including her.

Frantically she swam towards the jungle like the soldier had suggested. She scanned the nearby water for him but saw no sign of him amongst the debris and branches.

The edge of the wave was only ten metres ahead of her.

The water withdrew more slowly, dragging her with it.

She gasped and increased her effort, lungs burning, muscles aching.

Nearly there.

Mila reached out and her fingers brushed the smooth trunk of a palm tree.

One last stroke and the water shifted, slamming her against the next tree. Her breath evaporated, but she grabbed the trunk and curled her arms and legs around it.

She struggled to get air back into her lungs as the trunk began to creak and lean.

The water was ripping it out and trying to pull her

grip from the tree.

She sobbed as she scanned the wave's progress. Five metres, three metres, two metres.

An arm stretched in supplication out of it across the road in the jungle.

The soldier. He was alive.

For now.

She tried to keep track of him, but he disappeared beneath the water again.

The tree trunk was at a forty-five-degree angle now and still Mila clung to it.

The last of the wave washed past, and the tree stayed standing.

Mila couldn't let go. Her body was locked into position.

She exhaled, feeling every ache and pain in her body. Slowly she unlocked her ankles and let her feet fall to the ground, then she pried her fingers apart and slid to the dirt.

Her stomach retched, and she vomited dirty water all over the ground.

She panted, taking stock of the cuts and scratches on her arms and legs, the heavy bruises that were already forming. Slowly she moved each limb, checking for breaks.

Every cell of her hurt, but nothing was broken.

Safe. For the moment.

How quickly would the next wave come?

The fear forced her to her feet. She leaned against another tree to get her breath and then turned back towards the town.

Devastation.

Her raised vantage point up the sloped road revealed few buildings remained standing. Her little apartment was no longer there and the market square was full of rubble.

The scent of refuse, dirt and saltwater hit her, along with the screech and bang of buildings as the wave forced its way back to the ocean.

It would be a miracle if anyone survived.

She gasped. The soldier.

She had to find him. His team would be back for him and there might not be a lot of time before the next wave. "Can anyone hear me?" Her voice was raspy and she cleared her throat as she limped across the road and into the jungle. "Hello? Soldier man?"

Her whole body ached, and each step required her entire focus.

"Anyone?"

A moan and then a gurgling cough sounded nearby.

She moved further into the jungle. "Where are you?"

She followed pain-filled moans as if he was trying to be quiet but couldn't stop himself. She almost stood on the soldier, whose head was the only thing visible. The rest of him was covered in debris. Quickly she lifted and turned his head as he vomited a stomach full of tsunami water. When his retches stopped bringing up water, she lowered his head and shifted the leaves and branches from him. "Are you OK? What's your name?" His dark hair was knotted under her fingers. He was one of the men who'd helped her rescue Fajar's family.

"Ethan." He stuffed his fist into his mouth and groaned.

Her heart raced. He sounded as if he was in agony. He was hurt, badly. "Nice to meet you, Ethan." She kept her tone low and friendly. "I'm Mila. I'm sure your friends will be back pretty soon, so we need to get you out of here."

"Can't move."

Oh hell. Nothing covered his body. She hoped that didn't mean he was paralysed.

"We'll figure it out. Can you move your feet?"

"Pelvis," he gasped.

Shit. She knew nothing about broken pelvises. She reached for his hips and he pushed her away. "Go. The next wave won't be far away."

Fear gripped her and she glanced towards the ocean. "I'm not leaving you." He'd caught her, told her what to do when the wave turned. He'd given her hope. "What do you need?"

"Stretcher." The word ended on a wail and he shoved his hand back into his mouth.

There wasn't anyone around to hear... unless Agus was nearby. She dug into the bag still around her neck. She always kept a bucket hat inside in case she went into the sun.

She squeezed out the excess water and handed it to him. "Use this."

He stuffed it into his mouth and moaned around it, the pain striking her deeply.

"I'll find a stretcher." She wasn't strong enough to carry him, but she might be able to drag him.

Housing debris was littered around her; a piece of ceiling, a window frame... surely there had to be a door somewhere. "I'll be right back."

She marked a straight path from Ethan to the road so she could find him again and jogged down the cleared path before finally finding what she was searching for.

A wooden door lodged between two palm trees.

Mila yanked on it and it didn't budge. Come on. She had little time. She glanced back towards the ocean but couldn't see the wave any longer.

Quickly she moved around the other side and noticed vines tangled around it. She shoved at them but they didn't budge. What she needed was a knife.

Her hand tapped her bag and she grinned. Her mother had given her a multi-tool when she'd joined the army reserves. She'd never used it but kept it in her bag. She fished it out of her soggy bag and flicked the knife open, sawing at the vines until they sprang open.

Finally she dragged the door free. It was too large to get it under her arm, so she grabbed one side and dragged it back up the road.

"Quiet," Ethan called.

She smiled, relieved to hear his voice. "Be right there." She couldn't help the noise she was making.

The door got stuck on a few more things before she got it back to Ethan. She lay it next to him.

His eyes flickered open, and he removed the hat from his mouth. "Thanks, Angel." He groaned. "I don't feel so good."

"We'll get you on the door and I can drag you to the road so when your friends arrive you can ask them what took them so long."

A question she wanted answered. Surely they would be back for him.

She heard a car engine and hope filled her. "That will be your friends now. I'm going to flag them down and I'll be right back."

She moved back to the road.

Hopefully one of them was a medic.

Because Ethan needed a lot of help.

Fast.

Chapter 4

"We're clear!" Dobby yelled, staring out the back of the four-wheel drive at the dark wave of destruction, searching for the two people who had disappeared.

"The next wave might be bigger," Axle called. "We'll turn back and search for him when we get Vance to safety."

"No one would have survived it." Vance didn't seem cut up that the woman he'd been planning to marry had been swept away.

Arsehole.

Tension gripped every muscle in Dobby's body, but he couldn't turn around and face the front. He scanned the water, looking for any signs of life, even though they kept getting further and further away.

Finally the car stopped. "Joker, you and Radar take Vance into the jungle. You should be safe from any waves there," Axle said.

Dobby blinked and turned back. He should be giving the orders, but Axle was keeping his wits about him. Dobby nodded and the men got out.

"Don't go. Agus might come after us," Vance said.

"He's tucked up in his house," Dobby said. "He

won't leave until the danger is over."

"Aren't you all supposed to be protecting me?" Vance asked.

"One of our team is back there," Dobby said. "You can either stay in the car and join us searching the village or get out and stay with Radar and Joker."

Vance scooted over the seat and out the door.

Axle did a U-turn and Dobby sat in the middle of the back seat so he could see ahead.

Neither of them spoke as Axle tore back down the road, bumping over potholes.

The village finally appeared.

Or what was left of it.

Dobby stared out the windscreen at the devastation. How could anyone have survived?

He wanted to vomit. He'd had Hawk's hand in his and he'd let him fall.

A figure stumbled out of the jungle and the headlights illuminated her.

"Well shit," Axle said.

Dobby couldn't agree more. Mila was bedraggled, her clothes filthy and wet, sticking against her skin, but she was on her feet. If she had survived, then maybe Hawk had too.

She waved her arms, moving to the centre of the road so they couldn't drive past.

Not that they were going to.

"Have you seen Hawk?" Dobby called, pushing open the door.

"Ethan's through here. He can't move. He needs help."

Dobby leapt out and Axle turned the car around so it faced the other way before joining them.

They needed to get Hawk out of here before the next surge hit. Sometimes the second wave was worse than the first.

"This way." She shuffled into the jungle, one foot bare, the other still wearing a sneaker, and a soaked shoulder bag hanging across her body. "Did you get Vance?"

"Yeah."

"Is Agus coming after you?"

"Not until the tsunami clears." The man might have more vehicles at his disposal, but he was smart and wouldn't risk his own life to come after them.

"He's here." Mila crouched down next to Hawk.

Dobby squatted down. "Are you injured?"

Hawk opened his mouth but only a moan came out. He'd take that as a yes.

Mila had already cleared the debris from him. "He said he might have a broken pelvis. I found a door to transport him on. We have to go." She glanced anxiously towards the ocean.

Axle strode over. "Let me examine him."

"Pain," Hawk gasped.

Axle dug in his pack and pulled out his med kit.

Dobby cleared out of the way. He was impressed Mila had kept her wits about her and found a way to transport Hawk safely.

Axle examined Hawk for other injuries and gave him a shot of painkiller, while Dobby monitored the surroundings and cleared the area around Hawk so they could lay the door next to him.

No reaction while prodding his arms or his torso, but when Axle got to Hawk's hips, the man bellowed.

Axle snatched his hand away.

"Fuck off," Hawk gasped.

Dobby grinned, glad he was talking.

"Is that all that's broken?" Axle asked.

"Yeah."

"We need to get him on the door." Dobby collected some large palm leaves to work as a sheet to help drag

Hawk.

Axle looked up. "Let me get a splint around him first." He swung his pack off his back and reached into it, pulling out something he unwound and then slid under Hawk's knees and pulled up towards his hips.

Hawk stuffed something back in his mouth and bellowed around it as Axle tightened the splint in place. "Sorry. Let's get him out of here."

The car engine still purred nearby and Mila hurried to open the back doors.

As he and Axle carried Hawk to the road, he heard another sound. A dull roar.

The second wave was coming.

"Go." Hawk pushed him away.

"No chance." Dobby cleared their way through the jungle towards the car. Hawk gritted his teeth and moaned.

"We've got to move," Axle shouted.

"Copy."

As they reached the car doors, Mila ran to the other side so she could push down the back seats.

The roar grew louder.

Dobby placed Hawk's head and shoulders on the back bumper and then shifted to the side so he and Axle could push him the whole way in.

The wave was rolling towards them, picking up everything in its path.

The door just fit. Dobby slammed the back doors as Axle jumped into the driver's seat.

Dobby grabbed Mila's hand and dragged her on top of him as he slid into the passenger side. "Go."

The door hadn't even shut as Axle accelerated up the road.

Behind them the wall of debris was moving fast, getting closer.

Dobby's throat closed over. This was not happening

again.

Axle slammed through the gears and squealed up the road into the mountains.

Water sprayed from their wheels.

"Faster," Dobby barked.

The car lost traction and slid before Axle got control of it again.

Mila flinched and he realised he was squeezing her. He relaxed his hold. "Sorry."

"I get it," she whispered.

She must be terrified. She'd already been caught, but instead of fleeing to safety, she'd stayed to save Hawk.

The car surged forward and left the wave behind. It took another thirty seconds before Dobby stopped looking in the side mirror. He exhaled. "Good work."

"Thanks for coming back," Hawk murmured.

"I wanted to the first time..." Axle's voice held regret.

"You did the right thing," Dobby told him. This job was all about making the hard decisions and it was his fault Hawk had fallen.

"Thank you for saving me," Mila said, her voice soft. She trembled in his arms. He shifted so she could lean against his chest, ignoring her soaked clothing, and stroked her arm. She flinched.

"Are you injured?" He hadn't thought to check her.

"My whole body feels as if I've been in a washing machine on fast spin, but aside from bruises and scratches, I'm relatively unscathed." She started coughing, her body wracking, and she fumbled with the button on the window.

Dobby hesitated, wanting to stroke her back, but not wanting to hurt her any further. She seemed so fragile and yet so strong at the same time.

She spat water out of the window.

"How much water did you swallow?" Axle asked.

"A bit."

"Stomach or lungs?" Though Axle's question was casual, Dobby heard the concern behind it.

She finished coughing. "Stomach I think. I vomited a lot after the wave receded."

"We'll get you checked out by a doctor when we get back to the ship."

"Thanks." She shifted, peeling her shoulder bag from her body and placing it on the floor.

Her fragility sparked a flame deep in his gut and with it came anger. "What were you still doing down there? I told you to get out."

She flinched. "People needed help."

He opened his mouth to challenge her, but she beat him to it. "Should I have forgotten about Hawk and left him behind?"

The guilt hit him and he bit his tongue. "What happened to your moped?"

She squirmed and the movement came dangerously close to his crotch. He shifted slightly as his body reacted.

"Well?" he demanded, trying to keep his mind off the fact that her very thin sleep shorts weren't much barrier to her bare skin.

"An old woman stole it as I ran back to get a crying child. I got the child on the bike before the woman took off. The tsunami was almost on us."

He growled.

"My thoughts exactly," she said. "I had no choice but to run."

"You're lucky you survived," Dobby said.

"I know." Her soft words made him clutch her a little tighter as if he could protect her from the memory of what she'd been through.

"I'm Axle by the way," Axle said. "I'm guessing you're the ex?"

She nodded. "Mila." She glanced at Dobby.

"Dobby," he said and then winced. "At least that's what everyone calls me. My name is Damien."

Her smile lit up his world and then she glanced at Hawk in the backseat. He was silent, but his eyes were open, and he was watching them. "Have you got extraction planned?"

"We did," Dobby answered. "But it was by sea."

She winced. "Zodiac?"

He nodded. "We'll look for it when the waves subside."

Axle glanced over. "The ship was heading this way. Maybe we can get the chopper to come here. It will be incredibly painful to get Hawk out on a water extraction."

Good idea. The chopper wouldn't have as far to fly and now they could come to the island under the guise of aid.

"We'll get Radar to call."

Up ahead someone dressed in black stepped out on the road and flagged them down. Radar.

"Hawk's alive?" he asked as they pulled up.

"Yeah, but he's broken his pelvis." Dobby opened the door and waited for Mila to climb out before he joined her. "Where are the others?"

Radar gestured to the jungle. "Through there." He shook his head. "Vance is a piece of work. Keeps demanding we call a helicopter to pick us up."

Mila sighed. "That sounds like him."

Dobby scanned their surroundings. They hadn't passed anyone on the way and there was silence aside from the occasional bird call and the buzz of insects. "Get comms up."

Radar set up the antenna while Dobby found a survival blanket in his pack and wrapped it around Mila's dirty, scratched shoulders.

Mila smiled at Dobby. "Thanks."

"I can't offer you a shower yet," he said.

"I'm just thankful to be alive." She glanced to where Axle was examining Hawk in the back.

Dobby kept his arm around Mila's shoulder as Radar spoke with comms.

"Sun God, this is patrol six six, do you copy, over?"

"Patrol six six, this is Sun God. Send. Over."

"We've got a man injured," Radar reported. "Need immediate evacuation."

"Negative," base responded. "We have requests in. Base en route. Lay low. Check in on the down low."

Mila glanced at him. "What does that mean?"

Dobby growled. "Ship's en route, but they won't send a chopper until they get permission from the Indonesian government. We need to check back every half an hour." Fucking politics.

If Hawk wasn't injured, they'd easily be able to lie low in the jungle for a couple of days. They had enough rations and they'd camped rough before. But Hawk's injury was too severe to move him more than they had to. Dobby turned to Axle. "What does Hawk need?"

His gaze was bleak. "Surgery. The best I can do is stabilise him and give him some pain meds. The door is good because it's hard, stable and manoeuvrable, but it might be too wide in the jungle."

"Is there a medical centre in the village up the hill?" Dobby asked Mila.

"No. People come down here if they need help. The medical centre is first class thanks to Agus."

He stared down the road. The jungle blocked the view to the coast, but it would be suicide to go back now.

"Tell them I need to know the moment it's safe to go back," he barked at Radar. There'd be more waves to come.

He didn't want to move Hawk more than was necessary so the car was probably the best place for him to stay for now. But he needed to plan for eventualities. If Agus survived, he might head this way. "Axle, stay with Hawk. Radar, show me to the others." He turned to Mila. "Stay here for me. I need to check in and devise a plan."

He waited until she nodded and then followed Radar into the pitch black of the jungle, thankful he had night vision goggles.

About twenty metres in sat Joker and Vance. "Hawk?" Joker asked.

"Broken pelvis. He's in the car."

Vance stood. "Are you in charge? When are you getting me out of here?"

"Not tonight," Dobby told him. "You might as well make yourself comfortable."

"Here?" Vance sounded incredulous. "I'm not sleeping in the jungle."

Seriously? "I didn't say you had to sleep, but extraction isn't likely until daylight."

"I should have stayed at the house," Vance grumbled.

"You'd prefer to be with the kidnappers who threatened to kill you?" Dobby asked.

"No, of course not." He glanced away.

Dobby's bullshit metre went off the chart. He strode over to Vance and stood right in his face. "Why weren't you tied to a chair when we arrived?"

Vance stumbled back. "What?"

"In the ransom video your parents received, you were tied to a chair. Why did Agus let you out?"

"Ah…" Vance glanced around as if looking for a solution.

Which meant he didn't have an honest answer. Dobby's eyes widened.

"Did you fake the kidnapping?"

Vance's chest puffed up. Before he said anything, Dobby growled, "No bullshit. I have an injured, immobile soldier to protect."

"Aren't you supposed to be protecting me?"

"You are currently safe and uninjured. You are no longer my priority." He stared into the man's eyes, daring him to argue further. "Answer the question."

Vance stepped back. "Yes. No. At first."

Dobby clenched his teeth. "Explain."

"I needed money, and my selfish fiancée refused to marry me so I had to come up with something."

A flash of anger swept through him. "Mila Watkins?" He kept his voice deceptively light. "Your *ex*-fiancée?"

Vance nodded. "Yeah, well she'll be regretting turning me down now."

Dobby gritted his teeth. "You don't care she was caught in the wave?"

"She chose to be here."

He clenched his hands. How much trouble would he be in if he punched the man they'd rescued? It would probably be worth it.

"What did you come up with?" Joker asked, getting back to the point.

"When Mila said she wouldn't marry me, I told Agus my parents would pay crazy ransom money. All he had to do was send them a video of me tied up and when the payment came, he'd take a portion and I'd keep the rest."

Dobby almost laughed. "You thought he'd let you have anything when he could walk away with several million dollars?"

"He's rich. He doesn't need the money, but he wanted to help me."

Sure he did. "What happened after you sent the

video?"

"We waited. I didn't think they'd send you guys in. I figured they'd just pay it."

The man didn't deserve his parents who obviously cared deeply for him.

"Then the earthquake hit. Scared the shit out of me. I've never been in an earthquake before." Vance hugged himself. "Agus told me to chill. He'd built the house to the highest standards, whatever that meant. Anyway I chilled until one of his men ran in talking about a tsunami. I wasn't waiting around. That's when Agus locked me in the bedroom. He said the house would be fine and I shouldn't panic. He threatened to tie me up if I didn't behave." Vance shrugged. "There was something creepy about the way he said it."

Which was probably when Vance finally realised Agus wasn't as benevolent as he appeared.

"And now you've escaped?" Dobby asked. "Will he come after you?"

"He probably thinks I'm dead."

"He saw us rescue you." A couple of million dollars might be enough for Agus to search for him. "If he finds you, would he force you back to his house?"

"You guys won't let him take me."

"That's not what I asked. Is Agus likely to laugh it off as a joke, or shoot you for making a fool of him?"

The blood drained from Vance's face and Dobby had his answer. He turned to Joker. "We need to make a thinner stretcher."

Then they needed to ditch the car and hide.

Chapter 5

Mila watched Damien stride into the jungle and her body warmed. For those few moments when she'd sat on his lap, she'd felt safe and as if everything would be all right. But talk of extraction and the issues with Ethan's injury reminded her she was an extra on this mission, and they were under no obligation to rescue her. Her mother had spoken about how unplanned events often messed up a mission. She didn't want to mess this up for them.

She also wanted to know what the hell Vance was playing at. Had he genuinely been kidnapped, or had he realised she wouldn't marry him and implemented a backup plan? It wouldn't surprise her if he'd faked his kidnapping. He'd do anything to get out of doing any actual work. But once again he'd used her and dragged her into his mess. It was time to have words with him. Strong ones.

He'd taken away her option of staying here, enjoying living like the locals with their slower pace of life. She'd found her work deeply rewarding. The families who had welcomed her and helped her settle in had been so kind.

And now so many of them were left with nothing. How could she desert them when they needed her most?

But she couldn't stay when Agus clearly had a vendetta against her mother.

She curled up in the passenger side seat, wincing at her aches, while Axle spoke with Ethan.

When they set up camp, she'd ask if they had anything to clean her wounds with.

The only good thing to come out of this whole mess was Vance's father had sent in special ops, which meant even if they couldn't get her off the island with them, someone would know she needed help.

What assistance could she offer the team? Ethan needed medical attention fast. The medical centre in town was well stocked thanks to Agus and a famous surfer who had come for the surf and wanted to make sure they had the facilities he needed should he be injured. The break offshore apparently had a reputation.

But what state would the centre be in now?

Only one way to find out, but they'd have to wait for the waves to stop.

Her throat closed over at the thought of going anywhere near the coast. The hairs on her skin stood up, and she waved her hands to get some air movement around her.

"Are you all right?" Axle asked.

She nodded, swallowing hard. "Hot." That was also true. The brief relief from the humidity with the rainfall in the evening had been short-lived. The team didn't need to know she was close to breaking down. They might decide she was a liability.

Mila slowed her breathing, and her muscles relaxed. She had to get a grip. She was her mother's daughter. She could do this.

Calm. She knew this island better than they did.

What were their other options?

There were five villages on the coast and one in the mountain. Would the villages on the other sides have been affected as badly as this one? They might have a boat.

If they got out to deep water between the waves, they should be safe.

A slight rustling in the jungle had her glance over as Damien stepped out of the darkness. "Radar and Joker are building a thinner stretcher," he announced.

"Where are we going?" Axle asked.

"Nowhere yet," Damien said. "But chances are good Agus will look for Vance and we don't want to be sitting out here waiting for him." He glanced back at the jungle. "The door is too wide and awkward for easy manoeuvrability.

"How much fuel does the car have?" Mila asked.

"A quarter tank," Axle answered.

"That's enough to get across the island and do recon."

Axle's eyebrows rose and he smirked. "Recon?"

She refused to feel embarrassed. "The way I figure it, we either wait here until they get a chopper in, or we find a boat," Mila said. "The boats this side are either destroyed or out to sea. The other side might not have been hit as badly."

"A boat won't be great for Ethan," Axle said.

"Better than being shot," Mila replied.

"We might still have a boat," Damien said. "How far to the other coast?"

"You need to go over the mountain, so about an hour." She shrugged. "As long as there were no landslides from the earthquake."

"Radar and Joker can go when we've built the stretcher."

Mila rubbed her aching head. "What time is it?"

"Almost four." Damien rummaged around in his backpack and pulled out a packet. "Here."

Pain killers. "Thanks." She popped two out and swallowed them dry.

"Axle, can you check her over when you're done with Ethan?" Dobby asked.

"I'm fine."

"I'll check," Axle said. "Just in case."

Dobby smiled and helped her out of the car.

His smile warmed her insides. Now wasn't the time to be attracted to this man. He had a job to do.

Axle shone his torch over her arms and legs. He hissed at a gash on her forearm. "That might need stitches." He took his canteen from his hip and cleaned the cut. "When we get to camp, I'll clean all the cuts and put a couple of stitches in." He smiled in apology. "I'd like to check under your clothes as well."

She closed her eyes and nodded. He was a medic doing his job.

"Dobby, turn around and Ethan, close your eyes."

She doubted Ethan could see her from where he was, but she appreciated it when Damien turned his back to give her privacy.

Carefully Axle pulled up her top, and he winced. "It looks as if you've gone ten rounds with a prize fighter." He gently prodded her ribs and then turned her around so he could check her back. "You're lucky, but I'm worried about the water you swallowed. If you start to feel different, you need to tell me immediately."

She nodded. The thought of what could have been in the water was sobering and made her want to vomit again.

As Axle finished examining her, Radar returned carrying a stretcher made from wooden poles and some sort of fabric which they must have had in their packs.

"Where are we going?" Radar asked.

"We'll stay here," Damien said. "Close to the village if extraction comes. You and Joker can take the car and investigate options on the other side of the island."

"I'll clear a spot for Ethan." Radar glanced at Mila. "Come with me. I'll piggyback you."

She screwed up her face. "I can walk."

"I'm more worried about your bare foot getting injured," Radar said. "The jungle floor isn't the softest surface."

Damien nodded. "If we go into town, we'll find you something else to wear."

That would be good. The blanket was warm, but she was conscious of the fact she wasn't wearing a bra and her thin tank top hid nothing, particularly while it was wet. Thankfully it was still dark.

She grabbed her bag from the floor of the car. It was likely all that remained of her possessions. A wave of sadness passed over her thinking about everything the villagers had lost. Her possessions were nothing in comparison. She hopped onto Radar's back and he carried her through the jungle to where the man she assumed was Joker waited with Vance.

"Are we getting out of here now?" Vance whined as Radar walked into the clearing.

Typical.

"Not yet." Radar stopped, and she slid to the ground, wrapping the blanket back around herself.

"Why not?" Vance demanded.

Her patience snapped. She stepped out from behind Radar and said, "Because they have a man who broke his pelvis trying to save your sorry arse, and he can't be moved easily, so you'll have to wait."

Vance's eyes widened. "Mila. What happened to you?"

She scowled at him. "What? Other than the earthquake and almost being drowned by a tsunami?"

"Why didn't you get out of there?"

"Because people needed help," she replied. "I couldn't leave them stuck under debris." Helping others wasn't a concept he was familiar with.

"If I'd known, I would have got these guys to rescue you, I swear." He stepped forward as if to hug her and she ducked behind Radar to avoid him.

"Did you even consider where I was?" It shouldn't hurt, but his blank, slightly confused expression told her everything. She didn't wait for him to lie. "They didn't have time to rescue me," she said. "You only just made it out in front of the first wave." At his questioning look she added, "I saw you leave."

"Mila, baby, I'm sorry. I would never want you to be hurt."

"Other than forcing me to marry you or telling a known criminal how rich my father is?"

"I needed his help to get you back."

She raised her eyebrows. "Cut the bullshit, Vance. You don't care about anyone but yourself. You don't love me and you don't want to marry me." She blinked rapidly, glad it was too dark for anyone to see the tears welling in her eyes. She'd nearly died, and he didn't care. Why hadn't she seen it before?

"Sure I do. We'd be a power couple."

"Here on this island?" she asked sweetly.

"No. In Sydney."

"And if I want to live here?"

"No one would choose to live in this shit tip."

But she had, and he didn't get it. She closed her eyes. "Let me make this clear. I don't like you, let alone love you. I won't marry you."

Anger flashed across his face. "Don't be selfish. My father wants me to marry. It would only be for a couple of years. We were good together." He took two steps towards her and Radar shifted so he was standing in front of her.

Joker spoke. "Enough. The lady has said no. You will respect her decision."

His voice made her jump. What must they think of her?

"You're supposed to be saving me, not her."

"Trust me, mate," Radar said. "We're saving you from yourself and from her."

Joker chuckled. "Yeah. If you can't tell when a woman is mad, you're going to be in a lot of trouble in life."

"We need to clear a space for Ethan," Radar said as if that was the end of the matter and cleared leaves and branches out of the way.

Mila exhaled and unclenched her hands. She tied the blanket like a sarong around her breasts and helped, cautious where she trod so she didn't injure herself. By the time Damien and Axle carried the injured soldier into the clearing, the spot was ready. She shifted out of the way as they placed the stretcher on the ground.

Vance squeezed her shoulder so tightly she flinched. "We need to talk."

Almost without thinking, she elbowed him hard in the guts. "Take your hand off me."

Vance stepped away, his hands high. "Chill."

She exhaled, not wanting to cause a scene in front of Damien and the others. Radar murmured something to Damien, and Damien glanced across at her and nodded. Then Radar said, "We're up, Joker."

Mila stepped over. "The road winds its way up to the village and then down the other side. You can't get lost."

"Does it go through or around the village?"

"Through."

Radar frowned. "We'll have to scope it out first. If someone sees us, word might get back to Agus."

"There's a sign just before you get there on the left-hand side," she told them.

"Thanks."

Axle handed them a key. "Use this. It's programmed to the four-wheel drive."

"Copy." Joker tested the comms and then they strode out of the clearing. A moment later the car engine rumbled and then faded as the men drove away.

Axle crouched by Ethan, checking his vitals. Damien came over. "You both should rest. Nothing's happening until the waves stop which could be a few hours yet."

Now the adrenaline was waning Mila found herself swaying on her feet. Still she crouched next to Ethan and asked Axle, "Is there anything I can do to help?"

Ethan grabbed her hand and smiled. "There's my guardian angel. You remind me of my Chelsea." His voice was full of love with a slightly dazed drugged tone. "She was always so sweet."

Was. Who was Chelsea and what had happened to her? She winced at his tight grip and patted his hand, glancing with concern at Axle.

"I've given him the strongest drugs and made him as comfortable as I can." Axle smiled at her. "But before you rest, let me clean your injuries." He moved over to his med kit and gestured to her.

Gently she removed her hand from Ethan. His eyes were closed and his breathing was regular. Hopefully asleep.

Using a small torch for visibility Axle methodically cleaned each of her wounds, applying antiseptic to each one, chatting to her as he did so, but she needed a distraction from the pain. She murmured, "Who is Chelsea?"

Axle frowned as he cleaned her legs. "Ethan's ex. He doesn't see her anymore." He swiped a little harder on a cut and she hissed.

"Sorry. You're doing great."

It was hard to be upset at his calm, easy-going bedside manner, but she got the hint the topic was off limits. She appreciated he didn't want to gossip about his teammate. When he got to the gash on her forearm, he took a little longer to make sure the wound was clean. "I'm going to put a few stitches in."

She frowned. "I don't suppose you've got any anaesthetic in that kit of yours?"

He grinned. "Sure do. Don't worry, I've got you covered."

Mila turned her head as he got out a needle. Over on the edge of their makeshift camp, Vance was already lying down asleep.

Dobby was sitting with Ethan, murmuring to him.

"Just a little bee sting," Axle said.

She gritted her teeth as Axle injected the anaesthetic. It didn't take long for it to take effect and he sewed the gash and covered it in a waterproof bandage. "It's not as pretty as a plastic surgeon would do, but it shouldn't scar much." He packed his equipment away. "Rest now because we might have to move fast when it's time."

"All right. Thank you." She grabbed a few of the larger, less decayed palm fronds and lay them down to make a blanket of sorts. Damien helped her and then handed her a pack. "It's not bad as a pillow."

She smiled. "Thank you." It was kind of him to consider her comfort.

Vance grumbled something under his breath, so perhaps he wasn't asleep, but she paid him no attention. Then she lay down and the moment her head hit the backpack, sleep claimed her.

Chapter 6

Dobby watched as Mila fell asleep instantly. On the edge of the clearing, Vance was muttering and swearing. Dobby suspected he'd get pulled aside to deal with Vance's complaints after they were back in Australia. Not that he cared. The man was a selfish, privileged git, and not worth his time.

He'd been glad to hear Mila give him the serving he deserved, but he hated hearing the pain in her voice. Had she loved him?

Surely she hadn't been fooled by him. But perhaps he could be charming when he wanted something.

"She's a tough cookie," Axle murmured. "Her arm had to be hurting, but she didn't say a thing about it."

"She was more concerned about Hawk," Dobby agreed. Someone she'd only just met. It took a certain type of person to put strangers before herself. He felt drawn to her, but instead of moving closer, he stepped away. "I'm going to check the road."

Axle nodded as he made himself comfortable near Hawk, but between the road and the others.

Dobby crept through the jungle. Joker and Radar would have made sure they left no sign of them stopping there, but Dobby wanted to check. And he wanted to scope the surroundings, ensure there wasn't a rice field or houses near where they were camped.

He took his time watching the road to see if any survivors were leaving town and that people weren't returning to investigate things. He understood Mila's desire to stay and help. They'd be lucky if any buildings were left standing by the time the sun rose.

But he also had to keep to his mission, even if it had gone completely pear-shaped.

The insects had returned to chirping and a few birds squawked. The thick, rich scent of plants and decay filled his nose, a far more pleasant scent than back at the village.

Agus worried him and he didn't want Mila anywhere near him. If they were lucky, he'd stay holed up in his house until after they'd left the island, but he wouldn't count on that.

He'd keep her away from Vance as much as he could, too. Radar had told him what had happened. Dobby wouldn't let her be forced into anything.

Not that she seemed likely to give in to Vance.

Satisfied the road was clear and there was no sign they had been there, he circled the camp, creeping through the jungle listening for noises that shouldn't be there. He couldn't hear anyone speaking, or see any lights, which was good.

In the distance a macaque called and received an answering response. A few birds screeched, and a mosquito buzzed annoyingly close to his head. He swatted at it.

Shifting down the hill, he found a gap in the trees which allowed him to view the ocean. Another wave rolled in, but it didn't appear like it was too big. He made note of the time.

From his estimate they were maybe a bay around

from where they'd arrived. He sighed. He should have first sent Radar and Joker to scout for the zod in case by some stroke of luck it had survived intact.

But there was no fighting an enormous wave and the jungle was difficult enough to navigate through when it wasn't full of broken trees and debris.

The zod could wait, at least until they had a definite extraction time.

He stared down at the ocean. The water was littered with rubbish for almost a kilometre.

Even if they found a boat, it would be slow going through the debris.

As he stared at the water, he relived the moments the tsunami hit.

The way the wave had knocked Mila from her feet and buried her. Its onslaught as it caught up with Hawk and he disappeared from view.

The sudden knowledge it would be a miracle if either of them survived.

And he'd been helpless to stop it.

He shuddered and shoved it into a box to deal with later. Hawk and Mila had both survived. By Christmas they'd all be sitting around, having a beer and talking about the mission and laughing about what a douche bag Vance had been.

As long as Vance didn't decide he was better off with Agus.

Another wave rolled in and he checked the time. Yep. Thirty minutes. The crash of the wave against the shore reached him and he shivered. He shouldn't be able to hear any waves from this distance.

So definitely still tsunami waves.

He continued his round and when he was satisfied there was no one in the vicinity, he returned.

The camp was quiet. He gave Axle the all-clear signal. Axle gestured him over. Hawk was sleeping and

Axle moved towards him.

"I'm worried," he murmured. "Hawk might have internal bleeding. He needs surgery as soon as possible."

Shit. "Can you do anything for him?"

He shook his head. "It would be good to get some more pain medication for him and a hard stretcher so he's not jiggled about when we move him."

The only place they would get that was in the village. His gut clenched. "We need to get to the medical centre and discover what's left of it."

Axle nodded.

"Write me a list of what you need." They couldn't afford to wait for the all clear to be given.

"You can't go alone."

Dobby shrugged. It would be a couple of hours before Joker and Radar returned. "You need to stay with Hawk. It's thirty minutes between waves."

Axle frowned but nodded.

Yeah, Dobby didn't want to go back into the village if the waves hadn't stopped, but he would if it would save Hawk's life.

It was his fault Hawk was injured.

He ignored the tightening in his chest.

It was doable as long as he could navigate around the remaining buildings.

The rumble of an engine drew his attention.

It was too soon for Radar and Joker to be back unless they'd run into trouble. He crept towards the road, staying far enough back to ensure he wasn't seen.

The car was coming from the mountain. It slowed as it approached, flashed the headlights twice and then cut them.

Dobby slid his night vision goggles on and confirmed it was the black four-wheel drive. He stepped out, waved and Radar brought the car to a stop.

Radar wound down his window. "There are too many people awake in the village. We explored a little beyond it but there's a landslide blocking the road."

Which meant the other villages were cut off from them unless they found a boat, or trekked through the jungle.

"What should we do with the car?"

"Leave it there. We still need it." With the car, they'd reach the main village in only a few minutes. From there they might have to go on foot if the roads were blocked, which was highly likely. Another five minutes to reach the medical centre. Five to ten minutes to find the things they needed – if the centre was still standing – and another five to get back to the car.

Twenty-five minutes. That's what he needed between the waves.

He exhaled. Mila could tell him the location of the medical centre. "This way." He led the men back to camp.

He'd leave Axle and Radar with Hawk, Vance and Mila, and take Joker with him. Joker would have time to get to the beach where they'd left the boat and confirm whether it was still there.

But even if it was, getting out without hitting any debris would be difficult.

There was still so much that could go wrong with this damn mission.

And all for a selfish spoilt brat who would rather fake his kidnapping than work for a living.

He hated not being able to refuse a mission when it was something like this.

Dobby exhaled. No point dwelling on it. He still had to get his team and two civilians out of here safely.

Dobby went straight to Axle. "You've got my list?"

Axle handed it to him, shining a torch on it. "These

few things or the closest you can get to them," he said. "The rest is nice to have."

Dobby nodded, recognising everything from his medic training. "Waves are thirty minutes apart. I'll take Joker with me. Radar can keep contacting base. I just need Mila to tell me where the centre is."

"Or was," Axle pointed out.

Though it was a real possibility, it wasn't one he wanted to consider right now.

He crouched down to wake Mila. She was curled up, almost in the foetal position and lines creased her forehead. She wasn't relaxed in her sleep. He stroked her arm. "Mila, wake up."

Her eyes flashed open, and she jolted and then groaned.

"You're safe. It's Dobby."

She forced a smile onto her face. "Yeah. Sorry. My whole body aches."

Though concerned, he wanted to make her smile. "You think today's bad, wait until tomorrow," he joked.

She grimaced. "Thanks." She glanced around. "Are we going?"

"Not yet. I need to head to town. Where's the medical centre?"

"One street back from the beach, about two-thirds of the way along towards Agus's house." She sat up. "I can show you."

"No, you stay here. I'll find it."

She frowned. "If buildings have moved, I should be able to figure out where they've gone."

She had a point, but, "The all clear hasn't been given. I have to get in and out between the waves."

She stiffened and glanced over at Hawk. "It's bad?"

"He might have internal bleeding. Axle needs a few things."

She stood. "Then I'm coming. It will be quicker if

I'm your guide."

The woman had guts. She had to be aching all over and terrified, but her help would be invaluable. "All right. Let me get Joker." He checked the time. They'd wait until the next wave rolled in and then go.

He explained the plan and Radar sat up. "You three go to the car. I'll radio when the wave hits and you'll have a head start."

Good idea. "Thanks."

Dobby glanced at Vance who hadn't stirred during any of their discussion. Dobby leaned down to Radar. "Keep an eye on him. He might not be sleeping." And though there was nowhere for him to go, he was stupid enough to try something.

When he turned, Joker was already piggybacking Mila.

Dobby pushed down the jealousy that he didn't have her smooth legs wrapped around his waist.

He'd find her some shoes at the village.

Dobby drove them closer to town while Joker checked the comms.

"Wave's coming in now," Radar reported.

Dobby stopped at the closest point to where Joker needed to get out which was also just beyond the highest water mark.

The roar of the wave made him jump and Mila flinched. When Radar said, "It's receding," Joker jumped out of the car.

"See you in twenty."

It took no time to reach the edge of the town. Piles of debris were in every direction and the roads were blocked. Dobby drove as fast as he dared over the debris, hoping not to get a flat tyre until he couldn't go any further. He pulled the car off the road, turned it to face back up the hill and then got out. "Which way?"

Mila pointed.

As they picked their way across the broken wood, bits of coral and assortment of household appliances he put a gentle hand on her arm. "This isn't going to be pretty. We might see dead bodies or hear people calling for help. I need you to stay focused at least until we get to the medical centre."

She hesitated and then nodded. "All right." She hurried through the debris, shoulders slumping as she took in the total devastation.

Dobby's heart went out to her. She'd lost everything as well.

Mila hissed, hopping on her shoed foot and rubbing at her bare foot.

He scanned the area and trapped between two bits of wood was a muddy sandal.

He picked it up and handed it to her. "See if this fits."

Her smile lit up her face. "That's mine!" She slipped it on and did up the buckles. It would protect the bottom of her foot at least.

"Come on." They had to keep moving.

They had another hour before sunrise and the village was dark and silent. Mila moved with determination, climbing over roofs and walls, heading towards the beach.

Christ, the devastation was complete. A bomb wouldn't have destroyed this much.

It was starting to smell, a combination of dead fish, damp wood and forest decay.

As he followed Mila, his gaze roved. It was eerie how silent it was. He'd expected to see more death, but perhaps the residents had learnt from the last tsunami and hadn't stuck around after the earthquake had hit.

Closer to the coast, the way was clearer. The waves had pulled the debris with them and the ocean was now full of flotsam and jetsam. A lot of fish had been helpless to resist the force of the wave and had been stranded on land when it had receded.

"It's up here." Mila stepped around a pile of rubble. Her eyes widened. "It survived."

The building in front of them was the only concrete building in the town. The door had vanished and the glass windows were gone, but the building stood.

Now to discover whether the water had left any supplies inside.

"Let me go in first." He gently pushed ahead of her.

It was unlikely anyone would risk coming back before the all-clear, but someone might be as desperate as they were.

"All right."

He appreciated he didn't need to waste time arguing with her. The floor was damp and full of mud and rubbish. Anything on the shelves was gone, but at the back of the room was a door into a hallway. He scanned the ceiling. It wasn't just the tsunami that had hit. The earthquake may have done some damage as well.

He moved fast down the corridor. On the right was a treatment room with cupboards. The water still lay on the ground, but the cupboards were closed and a stretcher board was blocking the way.

Perfect. He passed the stretcher to Mila. "Can you carry this?"

"Yeah." She took it and tucked it under her arm like a surfboard.

Quickly he opened a cupboard and grinned. Bandages, all still in plastic packaging. He radioed camp. "Medical centre survived mostly intact. Be back soon."

"Copy."

He gathered what Axle needed, shoving it into his pack. "Let's go."

Mila turned to follow him from the room and the stretcher knocked against the bench, brushing items to the floor in a crash.

"Sorry," Mila whispered.

Dobby winced and held up a hand for her to stay still, waiting for the telltale sounds of someone coming.

He counted it out, mindful of the time they had before the next wave. Just as he was about to move forward he heard the pitter-patter of small feet. It took him only a second to place it.

Dog.

He pressed Mila back, putting her behind the door and placing a finger against her lips so she knew to stay silent.

She nodded, and he raised his rifle, waiting.

Voices called from outside.

Mila shifted closer, her breasts pressing into his side as she murmured, "They're calling for the dog."

For a second he was distracted by her closeness before his training kicked in. Agus's men didn't know where the dog was. That was a good start.

The dog crept into the treatment room, body low and tense. Would it remember the jerky he'd given it earlier?

Mila squatted, but he couldn't focus on what she was doing. If the dog attacked, he'd have to kill it, which would bring the other men into the medical centre.

Something splatted right in front of the dog. It jerked back and then sniffed at it.

A fish.

Mila had thrown it a fish.

Smart thinking.

The dog wagged its tail cautiously and picked it up.

Another yell, closer this time and the dog's ears pricked. It gave them another glance and then trotted out of the room with its prize.

Dobby exhaled, but still he waited as the voice yelled something else, followed by a thwack and a high-pitched yelp.

It was a weak man who hit an animal. He shifted, bringing Mila closer to his side, needing to know exactly where she was. They weren't out of danger yet.

Another yell and Mila gasped, and then her terrified whimper struck a chord deep inside him.

"What is it?" he demanded, his voice low.

"The next wave is coming. They're clearing out."

Shit. He squeezed her hand. "Let's get out of here."

He peered out of the door, scanning the front of the medical centre for movement.

Clear.

He motioned for Mila to follow him as they crept towards the door, Mila still carrying the stretcher under her arm.

Dobby reached the entrance and checked again for movement, but the dog and its handler were gone.

Behind him Mila was close to hyperventilating.

"Be brave and keep close to me," he murmured. "We're going to move fast as soon as the coast is clear."

"Dobby, where are you?"

Joker's voice sounded loud in his ear.

"A bit delayed. Car is about five hundred metres into the village." He placed Mila's hand on his shoulder. He gave it a reassuring squeeze and her breathing changed to longer breaths. She hadn't given in to her fear yet.

"Need me to fetch it?" asked Joker.

"Yeah." Hopefully the waves wouldn't be as big anymore and the car would be above its reach.

He shifted away from the medical centre, and as he cleared the back wall, he spotted two men with powerful torches, leaving the area.

They shifted the beams out to the ocean and the dog was a smaller shadow beside them.

Then Dobby spotted the receding water.

Shit.

Using such powerful torches was a disadvantage. Anything beyond the beam would be impossible to see as their eyes weren't adjusted to the darkness.

"We need to move fast," he murmured taking Mila's hand. "Stay out of reach of those torch beams."

And pray they didn't send the dog after them. He picked up two dead fish from the ground and handed them to Mila.

"Let's go."

She nodded and together they ran across the open ground. It only took a second before something they stepped on let out a loud crack.

Alarmed voices sounded behind them.

"They're ordering the dog to search," Mila whispered.

"Faster."

They sprinted over the low debris and then climbed over a mound. Behind them came more shouts, but the men weren't close enough to see them, and they were heading for high ground.

The dog on the other hand...

Its patter of paws was getting closer. Dobby turned as it launched its way over the mound. He raised his gun, praying he didn't have to use it.

A fish flew past him and almost hit the dog. It was enough of a distraction to make it stop, sniff the fish, and chomp into it.

Dobby grinned. "Good aim."

The dog sniffed the air and then wagged its tail with a little hesitation.

"Keep moving." He backed away, and the dog didn't follow.

The rumble of the wave was getting louder.

"Let's go." Dobby grabbed Mila's hand and dragged

her towards the car.

She called out something in Indonesian and he glanced back to find the dog following them and the wave had reached the beach.

Damn.

They stumbled over the debris and rubble.

The car was up ahead, but if Joker wasn't behind the wheel, the wave might still catch them.

"Joker, you at the car?"

"Yeah."

"We're coming in hot."

The engine roared to life.

"Give me the stretcher." He ripped it from Mila's hands. "Get in."

She ran to one side of the car, and he ran to the other. He threw the stretcher into the rear as she closed the door behind her.

"Go!" Dobby ordered as he leapt inside.

"The dog—" Mila shouted as Joker accelerated up the road.

Dobby shifted across the back area and pulled her into his arms, partially to soothe, partially to ensure she didn't jump back out in some daft rescue attempt.

"It's following," Joker said.

They both turned to watch the dog racing behind them, the wave at its tail. Mila sobbed, but the wave reached its peak and fell back, leaving the dog to continue after them.

"We need to lose it," Dobby said as Mila shuddered and started crying in earnest.

"You're safe," Dobby whispered, rubbing her back and soothing her.

He glanced up and saw Joker's sympathetic expression. They needed to get off this island. "Boat?"

"The tree it was tied to is gone, but I couldn't find evidence of it being torn up. Might have been dragged out to sea."

Damn. It was what he'd expected but it would have been nice to have the option open.

Mila's sobs lessened. "I'm sorry. I'll get it together in a second."

He brushed a kiss against her hair. "Take the time you need. That was some scary shit."

She laughed and hiccupped. "You weren't scared."

"Sure I was." Pleased she was talking, he kept his tone friendly. "Joker, Mila saved our arses by feeding the dog."

She made a sound of disbelief. "Hardly."

"No, really. If the dog is properly trained, it's told to bark when it finds what it's searching for. You throwing the fish to it distracted it. We could have been stuck in the medical centre fighting off Agus's men while the wave rolled in."

Mila stiffened, then let out a shaky breath.

"Sounds bad ass," Joker said.

Dobby flashed him a thankful smile. "High praise."

She raised her head from his chest and suddenly they were eye to eye only inches apart.

Her sharp intake of breath had nothing to do with fear. Neither did the tightening in his body.

The urge to kiss her was overwhelming. He leaned forward and the car braked, throwing him off balance.

He glanced at Joker.

"We're here," Joker said. "Get the supplies to Axle and I'll ditch the car."

The mission. He had to keep the mission in the forefront of his mind and not be distracted by his attraction to Mila. "I'll go. You take Mila to camp." Some distance might clear his head.

Mila opened the car door, but she touched his arm. "Be careful."

Her concern warmed his insides. She was far too

appealing. He nodded and gave the stretcher to Joker.

He scanned the road. No sign of the dog. Hopefully it had returned home.

Joker led Mila into the jungle and Dobby accelerated away. Now he needed to find somewhere to leave the car. Ideally he'd find a spot to hide it, but the road was narrow and the drop offs were steep. He was about three kilometres from camp when he spotted a gap in the trees.

The ground was sloped, but not on an angle that would cause the car to roll. He folded in the side mirrors with a touch of a button and drove in as far as he dared. Before getting out he checked they hadn't left anything inside and then quietly closed the door. He walked back to the road to check how well it was hidden and then used his knife to cut a couple of fan palm leaves down and place them strategically over the back. It wasn't pretty, but most people wouldn't be taking their eyes off the road to notice it.

He made note of the coordinates and then jogged down the road back to camp.

Now he had to get them off this island.

Chapter 7

Mila's heart continued to race as she followed Joker back to the camp, but she wasn't sure whether it was because she'd been certain they were going to be swept up by the wave again, or because of the moment she'd shared with Damien.

The intensity in his eyes, the way he'd held her so tenderly, his soothing words when she'd been close to meltdown, replaying being sucked under the wave over and over in her head.

She placed a hand on her heart as Joker set down the stretcher next to Ethan who even in the dark looked pale. He smiled at her. "Hey, Angel. I thought I imagined you."

Oh. He was still high on the drugs. She squeezed his hand to soothe herself as much as him. They were all safe. "I'm real. How are you feeling?"

"OK. It doesn't hurt anymore."

"Good. I'm glad." The others were waiting to see to Ethan, so she returned to the spot where she'd been sleeping and focused on her breathing.

Radar and Joker gathered around Ethan and helped Axle.

Mila wrapped her arms around herself, despite the humid night. When she'd offered to go with Dobby, she hadn't considered Agus's men might be down there.

She frowned.

Why had they been down there? It was still dangerous, and it wasn't as if there was anything of value to salvage.

Perhaps they'd heard the car and been sent to investigate. She hadn't heard any other engines, so they'd probably been on foot with the dog.

Her chest tightened and she exhaled to ease the tension.

The dog had survived. Seeing it sucked under by the wave would have been horrific.

She shivered and wrapped her arms around her.

"Cold?"

She jumped at the voice and looked up at Joker who had picked up her silver blanket and was holding it out to her.

She wasn't, not with the thick sultry night air and the adrenaline pumping in her body, but she accepted it. "Thank you."

He offered her a protein bar and sat next to her. "Can you tell us what happened?"

Mila glanced around the clearing to find the team watching her. Of course, they didn't know. She explained about running into the guards and distracting the dog.

Joker sighed. "The dog was half starved. People like Agus seem to think a hungry dog makes a good attack dog, but it doesn't."

"Did they see you?" Radar asked.

"I don't think so. How's Ethan?"

Axle glanced up. "These things will help. He's stable at the moment."

"Any news from base?" she asked.

"Nothing new," Radar answered. "With the boat out of the running, our best chance is via helicopter as soon as they get permission. Is there a clearing somewhere away from Agus's house?"

Mila pursed her lips. "How much space do you need?"

"About the size of two tennis courts. Best case we want it to land because it will be quicker and easier to board with Hawk."

The square would have been ideal, but it was covered in rubble now. "The village on the south coast has a soccer pitch and all the villagers play games there once a month."

"The road is blocked," Joker said. "We have to carry Hawk. Anywhere closer?"

"When the tide goes out, the beach is clear." She sighed. "But not today."

Joker nodded. "What else? Just throw out ideas even if you think they won't work."

"Anywhere else they play soccer or field games?" Radar asked.

"Each village has a market square, but chances are high they're all destroyed." She bit her lip. "And the easiest way to get to the villages is by boat."

"Are there any roads?" Joker asked.

"There's a dirt track running from the main road to each village, but they're rough and they always get washed out in the wet season. People travel by boat at this time of year."

"This just keeps getting better and better," Radar grumbled.

"The best place is Agus's cliff," Mila said. "It's a clear area and it's close. Perhaps there's some way we could lure him away and land there."

Joker grinned. "I like the way you think. Will he

leave to check on anyone in the village?"

She shook her head. "All of his family lives with him."

"We think he sent them away on his boat," Joker said.

"Vance might know for sure," Mila said.

They all looked over to where he slept. Radar stood and tapped him on the foot. "Wake up, Vance."

Vance groaned and grumbled.

"Do you want to be rescued or not?" Radar barked.

Vance sat up, brushing his long fringe out of his face. "Are we leaving?"

Radar grinned at him, wolfish and a little gleeful. "Not yet. We're planning and we need your help."

"Isn't planning your job?" Vance yawned, then he spotted Mila and straightened. "What do you need to know?"

"How many people does Agus have in his house?"

"I don't know."

Mila rolled her eyes. "Did anyone leave after the earthquake?"

Vance nodded. "Yeah. Everyone gathered downstairs and Agus sent the women and children to his boat. He wouldn't let me go with them."

"What about his bodyguards?"

"He always has two men with him so I guess they're his bodyguards."

"What about weapons?" Axle asked.

"His guards carried rifles," Mila said. "There were four that I saw."

"We injured a couple during the rescue," Joker said. "So the two men you saw in the village might be all he has left aside from his bodyguards."

"We can handle four armed men," Radar said.

Axle spoke up. "Not if the helicopter is coming in on the pretence of aid. We go shooting people now and there'll be questions."

They didn't need an international incident.

"If they're dropping aid, Agus will want to take what he can in order to control the people," Mila said. "So we need to get him out of the village so he can't get back in time." She glanced at Radar. "Are they bringing aid?"

"I don't know. That's the excuse they'll use to fly in here."

She hoped they would. The only thing that would lure Agus from his home was money, and he'd lost out when they'd rescued Vance. He'd be bitter about that.

But then there was one other money maker on the island. Nerves fluttered in her stomach. She hated to suggest it, but it was their only option. She glanced over at Ethan, remembered his firm hold on her arm as the wave pushed them around. The determination in his gaze that had given her hope. This was her way to repay him. She would figure out another way to escape. She stiffened her spine. "There's one thing that might lure him out."

"What's that?" Joker asked.

"Me."

***

Dobby walked into the clearing in time to hear Mila offer herself as bait. Anger spiked. "No fucking way." Not for Vance. He didn't deserve her sacrifice.

Radar lowered his weapon as he recognised Dobby. "You ditch the car?"

"Hid it three ks up the road on the right-hand side." He gave them the coordinates.

"Great," Joker said. "Now how about you take a seat and listen to Mila's suggestion before you reject it?"

Dobby scowled at him.

"You haven't heard everything we've been

discussing."

He sat next to Mila. "I'm listening."

She swallowed hard. "Agus doesn't know I'm with you." She glanced at him. "We're pretty sure the guards didn't get close enough to see us, right?"

He nodded reluctantly. "Best they would have seen is two shapes running away."

"So Agus is going to think either you've left the island, or it's too dangerous to go after you. You've already injured some of his men." She took a deep breath as if bracing herself. "He hates my mother. She had him arrested twenty years ago and ruined his marriage to the chief's daughter. He wants to punish her, and now he knows who I am."

They all glanced at Vance, but he just stared defiantly back.

"We can set up the extraction at the cliff top," Mila continued. "While you head there, I'll make my way to the village of Desa Agung at the top of the mountain." She pursed her lips. "Maybe I can take the car and say I found it abandoned. I'll tell people the wave knocked me unconscious, which is why I'm only just arriving."

He didn't like that she was making fantastic points.

"And how is Agus going to know you're there?" Joker asked. "Phone lines are down."

"He has loyal men at each village. The last time I was in Desa Agung I was visiting a family and heard the father talking to him on the radio. I can ask him to contact Agus. Say I'm worried about Vance and want to make sure he's safe."

Smart, and something Agus would believe.

"And how is Agus going to get there? We stole his car," Radar pointed out.

"He's got two four-wheel drives and several off-road motorbikes," Vance piped up. "He showed me his garage when I was there."

Finally the man was being useful.

Mila looked at Dobby. "I just need to figure out how to time everything so Agus doesn't get the call until we know when the chopper is coming."

She was missing one thing. "What about you?"

"I'm not your mission." Her smile was sad. "I know you'd take me if you could, but I'll figure something out."

"You expect us to leave you behind while we get extracted?" Dobby asked. Not happening. The rest of his team were shaking their heads, too.

She shrugged. "The road to the northern coastal village is just before Desa Agung. I can drive there after I confirm Agus has left and maybe the chopper could swing by there to pick me up." She glanced at Joker. "It wouldn't need to land, would it? Someone could throw down a ladder. I've seen it done in movies."

Dobby growled. "This isn't the fucking movies."

Joker slapped him on the shoulder. "It isn't, but it would work."

"It's dangerous, and we don't know when we're getting the all-clear." A weak argument, but he didn't want Mila risking herself. She'd been through too much already.

The blacks and greys of the night were shifting into colours defining his team more clearly. First light wasn't far away. "I'll go with you."

"You can't. If you're seen, Agus will know the team is still on the island. You need to be with the others. With two of you carrying the stretcher, you'll need two people to defend them and Vance if you get spotted."

He hated she was making very valid points.

"We'd make it work," Axle said.

Good. Finally some backup.

"I have to go in alone," she insisted. Her face was a picture of determination and damned if he didn't admire her more for it.

Radar held up a hand to stop the arguing. "It's time I called base. They might have an update."

Dobby nodded his assent, his gut tensing. It went against everything he was to let a civilian risk herself for a mission.

Particularly when the civilian was as kind and selfless as Mila.

Mila got to her feet. "I need to use the bathroom." Her face flushed.

"Don't go too far," he told her.

"I won't."

Radar established a connection. "Looking for a sitrep."

"All clear about to be given," the operator said.

"What about extraction?"

"Expecting to hear from the Indonesian government at oh six hundred."

Dobby checked his watch. Soon. Good. He wanted off this island.

"Best extraction zone is the cliff area on the west coast," Radar said.

What the hell was he saying? They hadn't agreed to that. He reached for the radio and Joker shoved him back.

"He's right. It's the safest location. There's too much debris in the town."

"Copy that," the operator said. "How's the patient?"

"Drugged," Radar replied. "We'll need space for six and a stretcher."

"Six?"

"Picking up Major-General Watkins's daughter as well," Radar explained.

Dobby exhaled. Good.

"Standby for extraction time."

"OK, we need ideas on how to get Agus away from

his house," Dobby said. "Mila saved a bunch of people. Maybe we can get one of them to tell Agus she's with them."

"She won't do it." Hawk's voice was weak.

Dobby moved over to him so he didn't need to speak loudly. "Why not?"

"Because Agus's wrath would come down on them when he discovers they lied."

Damn it. He was right. "How are you feeling?"

"Like I've been hit by a truck."

"Not long now and you'll have the best pain meds the army can buy."

He grimaced and Dobby laughed.

The radio crackled. "Extraction has been green lit. Extraction time oh eight hundred."

"Copy that," Radar replied.

Two hours. He could drive Mila to Desa Agung and they could use a moped to return to town. They could hide on the side of the road when Agus drove past.

It was weak, but he was coming up empty on other options. "Let's pack up."

He glanced around the clearing. There was plenty of light, but Mila wasn't there. He checked the time. She'd said she was going to the bathroom over fifteen minutes ago. "Where's Mila?"

The others looked around.

"She's gone to the mountain village," Vance said.

Dobby swore. "What do you mean?

The man shrugged. "She said it was the best option."

Dobby clenched his hands. "Why didn't you stop her, or tell one of us?"

"Because it is the best way. You weren't here to save her."

He growled and Radar slapped a hand on his chest to stop him doing something stupid, but even Joker stepped forward before he caught himself.

This prick wasn't worth saving, but they had a job to do. He clenched his jaw so hard it hurt.

Axle spoke. "Go find her. You've got about an hour and a half before we need Agus gone from his house. We'll head for the cliff clearing and we'll swing by the northern beach to get you if you don't make it to the cliff."

Radar pressed something into his chest. "Take the sat phone just in case."

Used for emergencies only. "Copy." He grabbed his pack and strode away.

There was a selfless, frustrating woman he needed to have words with.

Chapter 8

Mila wished she'd had time to bandage her foot before she'd left the camp. The sandal protected her sole but branches scratched every area that wasn't covered—which was most of it. She'd grabbed a couple of bandages from the medical centre for that purpose, but didn't dare stop now in case the team caught up with her.

She just hoped the cuts didn't get infected by some weird jungle disease.

Her breath came in pants as she strode up the road. She figured she'd have about fifteen minutes before anyone noticed she was missing.

Vance wouldn't dob her in. He'd come after her when she'd left and told her she had a solid plan.

She shook her head. He'd been so earnest, as if she was the only one thinking clearly and the special ops guys didn't know what they were doing.

But she saw through his bullshit now. He was only interested in saving his arse and she was a means to that end.

He didn't see the irony that she was putting herself in harm's way because of him, because of the information he'd shared with Agus.

She exhaled, pushing away her anger. She wasn't doing this for him. She was doing this for Ethan and Damien, the men who'd risked their lives to come here.

Ethan needed to be off this island with as little fuss as possible.

And Damien... well something about him was special. He exuded confidence and a protector vibe that made her want to climb into his arms and stay there.

He was a man worth fighting for. He had argued against her putting herself in harm's way, not encouraged it.

She jogged up the road, her steps loud in the morning's stillness. The dawn brought pastel colours to the surroundings.

She had no illusions that if the men disagreed with what she was doing, they would catch up with her. She'd never been a jogger and after the night she'd had, she wasn't at her best.

Damien would realise this was the only option. He had to put his team first, and by her leaving, she was taking the decision out of his hands.

He didn't have to feel guilty about it.

Shadows were fading and the drop off on the side of the road was clear. Hopefully the car wouldn't be hard to spot. Mila was hopeless at estimating distances and had nothing to check coordinates, but the fan palms covering the back should be noticeable going this slowly.

She kept listening for any motors. If the all-clear had been given, it wouldn't be long before news would filter through to the villagers and they'd return home to take stock of the damage.

Agus would only inform them after he was certain there wasn't anything he wanted in the village.

Not that there was anything left to steal.

At a rustle behind her, she turned. The road was empty and so was the forest beyond. It was probably a bird.

She turned and thumped into something warm and solid.

"Ow." Pain spread through her as she took in the dark fatigues, broad shoulders, tanned neck and the angry expression on the very attractive face of Damien. Damn. She hadn't realised how blue his eyes were. They were the type you wanted to dive into and swim around in, even if they were not impressed right now.

Her heart raced and she smiled. "Hi."

His pissed off expression didn't change. "Did you really think you'd get far?"

"Well I'd hoped to get a little further."

He growled, and she stepped around him and kept walking. He grabbed her arm. "Mila, I'm not letting you sacrifice yourself."

Her stomach clenched. She didn't want to be stuck on this island with Agus, but Ethan's life was more important. She was almost certain she'd be able to evade capture in the village.

"Damien, this is the best way and you know it."

The pain in his eyes spoke to her, and she placed a hand on his cheek. "Ethan needs help and you don't want to be shooting at people while trying to get him onboard." She ran her thumb over the roughness of his day-old stubble and he grabbed her hand to stop her.

Yeah, that was inappropriate, but she wanted to keep touching him.

"You've been through enough."

Did he feel this pull of attraction too? "I'm tough. I can handle it."

His lips turned up. "I have no doubt you can." He shifted closer. "I don't want you to. I don't want to risk you."

Her heart fluttered. "I'll be fine. I promise." She brushed a kiss against his lips to seal her vow.

His sharp inhalation made her think she'd made a mistake and then his lips crashed against hers.

Passion, lust, fire.

His tongue slipped between her lips and she moaned.

This. This was what she'd been missing from the other men she'd kissed. A passion that promised he would do anything for her. He pulled her closer, his hand pressing on a sensitive bruise and she winced.

Instantly he stepped back. "I'm sorry."

"Don't be." She swayed towards him but kept her feet still. "You touched a bruise." They didn't have time for this, as much as she wanted it. "I need to go."

"I'm coming with you," Damien said.

She shook her head, but he was already speaking into his comms. "I've found her."

Someone must have responded because Damien replied, "Copy." He turned to her. "I'll fetch the car. You keep moving, but if you hear anyone, get off the road and hide."

"Is there enough space to turn around on the road?" she asked.

"I'll figure it out." He hesitated. "Be careful. If you get worried, hide until I return."

"I will. You be careful."

He kissed her briefly and then turned and jogged up the hill.

She touched her lips. Wow. That had been unexpected, but she wasn't complaining. He was an incredible man. She enjoyed watching his butt as he jogged up the hill.

So that's what being super fit looked like. He disappeared from view before she remembered she was supposed to keep walking.

When she got home, fitness was going to be a priority.

She lengthened her stride as she followed the road.

Wait.

Her steps slowed. They wouldn't leave Damien behind. Perhaps they would pick them up on the northern beaches like she'd suggested.

Relief filled her. Either way she wouldn't be stuck here alone.

She closed her eyes and took a moment to be grateful to these men.

She was going home.

The morning was still as if it wasn't sure whether the destruction of the night was over. No wind rustled through the trees and even the birds had stopped their chirping. The only sound was her constant steps on the bitumen road which sounded far too loud.

Mila glanced behind her, but the road was empty. The rainforest trees towered above her, shading the road and blocking her view of the ocean and Batara below.

It was maybe fifteen minutes later when the rumble of an engine reached her. She twisted to figure out it was coming from above her. The mountain to her left dropped away, and to her right it was an almost vertical incline. Crap.

If it wasn't Damien returning, she'd be seen.

She ran forward to the bend in the road where the drop off wasn't as steep and ducked behind a tree, clinging on to it as a black four-wheel drive reversed down the road.

Damien.

She stepped out, waving him down and he stopped, and got out.

"Did you reverse this whole way?"

He nodded. "No way to turn around. You need to

drive."

"Why?" She got into the driver's side and adjusted the seat.

"Because you're right. No one can see me with you. Before we get to the village, we'll hide the car and hike the rest of the way. I'll wait in the jungle and watch what's going on. You stay out in the open, do not go inside. Does this village have a square as well?"

She nodded.

"Then stay there. Tell them you're too scared to go inside in case another aftershock hits."

She could do that. "Do we need some sort of bat signal?"

His low chuckle warmed her. "You mean an emergency signal?"

Heat flooded her cheeks. "Yeah. Some kind of shit's just gone south and we need to run, kind of signal."

He sobered. "I hope it doesn't come to that."

So did she. "So after I ask them to call Agus to check on Vance, I'll ask Agus to bring him to me, say I need to see him, but I'm too scared to go near the ocean. He won't admit Vance isn't with him. Then I can sneak out of town, and we can go to the extraction point."

He touched her arm. "Yeah, but here's the thing. Plans go sideways all the time. If something happens, stay calm. Do not risk your life. Just know I'll be coming for you."

The declaration hit her in the heart and stole her words. She nodded.

They drove in silence until a moped appeared on the road in front of them. Damien ducked.

"We're close," Mila said. "That was Fajar's father." She glanced in the rear-view mirror to make sure he hadn't turned around. "They must have been given the all-clear to return."

"Stop here." He checked his watch and frowned.

"What is it?" She pulled off to the side before the sign which announced the village.

"We're earlier than I'd like us to be. It'll only take Agus forty to fifty minutes for a round trip. That means he could get back to his house before the extraction." He got out. "Take your time walking into the village and before you ask to contact Agus. I'll turn the car around and meet you there."

"Should I wait for you?"

He grinned. "I'll catch up. We have to be out of the village by oh seven thirty at the very latest."

"I don't have a watch."

"Find someone who does." He stood at her window waiting.

This was her plan. She just didn't like the bundle of nerves in her stomach as she got out.

"I'll be right there with you," Damien promised and brushed a kiss on her cheek.

His declaration filled her with confidence. Mila headed for the village, walking the few hundred metres from the sign to the square.

Not as many of the longhouses here had been damaged. Groups of people congregated around cooking fires in the square and children slept on the ground where there was space. She spotted people from her village and those who lived here. An area had been set aside for the injured and the doctor from the medical centre was seeing to them.

Men were already sorting the debris into what could be reused and what would have to be disposed of.

Mila clenched her hands. She wanted to help these people, but how could she?

There were a few shocked glances when they noticed her.

She must look a mess with her hair in knots and

wearing filthy pyjamas. Mila exhaled, calming her nerves as she scanned the people for the man who worked for Agus, Ibu Minar's son, Patar.

"Mila!" Fajar's mother called and ran over to her. "I was so worried! Thank you for saving us."

Mila hugged her back, tears welling in her eyes.

"Where have you been? Are you all right?"

She didn't need to fake her exhaustion. "I got caught by the wave." She followed Fajar's mother over to a fire. "I must have lost consciousness. When I woke I was in the jungle."

Fajar's mother pressed a bowl of rice porridge into her hands.

"*Terima kasih.*" She took a mouthful and sighed at the warmth. Much better than the protein bar she'd had.

People crowded around her.

"Have you seen the village?"

"Did you find anyone else?"

She shook her head in response to the second question. "It's taken me all night to walk here."

"You must be exhausted," Fajar's mother declared. "We'll get the doctor to check you over."

"Where did you get the bandage?" The loud demand silenced the rest of the voices.

Mila glanced up at the man who had pushed his way to the front of the crowd. Patar.

Shit. "I got it from the medical centre. I was bleeding badly and timed it in between the waves." As long as he didn't make her take it off and see the stitches, she'd be fine.

"The medical centre is still there?" someone asked.

She nodded. "It's the only building still standing."

People gasped and a few sobbed, but Mila kept her attention on Patar. "Where's Agus? Is my friend Vance here?"

"We have not seen Agus or your friend," Fajar's mother said.

"Did you see anyone in the village?" Patar demanded.

She shook her head. "I didn't look. I was terrified I'd get caught in the medical centre when the next wave hit, so I went straight there and then headed up the mountain." She glanced around. "Maybe Agus stayed at his house. Have you heard from him?"

Patar hesitated. "Yes. Agus is safe."

"Good." Mila faked her relief. "Is my friend with him?"

"I don't know." The man stepped back, his expression a little wary. Agus had obviously told him something.

Fajar's mother frowned. "There are a few people missing. They may have left on their boats to deeper water. Where was your friend staying?"

"I thought he was staying with Agus." She had a part to play. She stood, wincing as she did so. "What time is it?"

"Almost seven."

Still a little early to ask Patar to call.

"How bad is it?" Fajar's mother asked. "In the village?"

"Bad," Mila admitted. "It's mostly piles of debris."

Tears appeared in the woman's eyes and Mila hugged her. "We'll work it out."

Across the square she spotted Ibu Minar, the woman who had stolen her moped. She was lying on a makeshift bed watching Mila. Guilt crossed her face as Mila caught her eye and she looked away.

Mila didn't have the strength to be mad. It had been a terrifying situation. But it meant her moped should be around here somewhere. She scanned the square and spotted it tucked along the wall of the house Ibu Minar was lying in front of.

If she couldn't sneak out of the village, maybe she could ride out.

Would Agus search for her if he arrived and she'd gone? Or would he head straight back to his house?

This was a lot harder than she'd expected. She casually looked around, trying to spot Damien in the jungle. Nothing. Maybe he hadn't made it yet.

She would have perhaps fifteen minutes to escape after Patar confirmed Agus was on his way. Any longer than that and she would risk running into Agus on her way down the mountain.

"You didn't see the men in black?" Patar asked.

His words shocked her out of her thoughts. "What?"

"Ibu saw you talking with men in black when she was trapped." He gestured to his mother.

Shit. Maybe Ibu Minar had been conscious longer than Mila had realised. "They appeared out of nowhere and then disappeared."

"Did they speak to you?"

"They asked how they could help."

"Anything else?"

"No. They helped lift a couple of things and then left. I assumed they were heading for another part of the village to search for survivors." Mila met Patar's eyes, knowing she was a terrible liar but also knowing if she looked away she would seem like she was lying. She needed a distraction. "Is it too early to call Agus?" she asked Patar. "I want to know if my friend is safe."

A pause as he studied her and then he said, "Of course. I'll contact him now."

"Thank you."

Mila moved closer to Patar's house but stayed outside, eating her bowl of porridge. She couldn't hear the conversation inside.

Patar came out of the house carrying a radio. "Your friend is with Agus and is safe. Agus asked me to accompany you back to the village."

"No!"

The man frowned at her outburst and she frantically thought of an excuse. "I can't go back there." She stepped away from him. "Not until the all-clear. It's too dangerous."

"The all clear has been given."

She backed further away. "I won't. Ask him to bring Vance to me. I can't go back yet." She forced herself to take heavy, panting breaths as if she was having a panic attack, and let Fajar's mother help her into a seat.

"It's safe," the man said.

Mila shook her head. "No. If Agus isn't leaving, then it isn't safe. He knows what's going on." She hoped appealing to Agus's ego would work and wouldn't tip him off that she was lying through her teeth.

She needed him out of town. She hadn't even considered he might not come for her himself.

Foolish.

What could she say to get him here? She scanned the square hoping to spot Damien, but he was nowhere to be seen.

"Ibu, I assure you it's safe."

"No. I can't go near the water." She hugged herself and rocked a little, not having to fake her nerves.

The man scowled and spoke into his radio. "She's too scared to go back."

"Bring her to me."

She glanced around, frantic to find an excuse. "I can help here." No, that wouldn't work. Agus might think she was occupied and not bother coming until he was ready. "Tell him I'm ready to marry Vance, but I want to do it here."

Patar relayed the message.

Though it was a lie, the thought of marriage made her think of her mother. "Does anyone have a phone? I want to tell my mother I'm safe."

"Mila!" Ibu Minar waved her over. "Patar has a phone." She waved imperiously at her son.

Mila swallowed her smile. Perhaps the woman wanted to make amends. She walked over to Ibu Minar. "I'm glad you're all right. How's your foot?"

"The doctor has set it." Ibu Minar grabbed her hand. "I am so very sorry."

Mila patted her frail skin. "It's OK. I am safe."

"Fetch the phone!" the woman yelled to Patar.

Patar waved his acknowledgement and said to Agus, "She wants to call her mother."

"No!"

Mila pretended she didn't hear Agus's explosion.

"I'll be there soon," Agus said.

Elation filled her. She handed Fajar's mother her empty bowl. "Thank you so much."

"Thank you. You will always have a place in my home." The woman hugged her. "You saved my family."

Tears pricked in Mila's eyes. "I couldn't have left them. What is the time?"

Fajar's mother pursed her lips. "Quarter past seven."

Fifteen minutes before she had to leave.

"Fajar told me about the men but I didn't tell Patar," Fajar's mother whispered.

Mila stared at her in shock.

"Neither did Ibu Sari. Fajar told me Ali took your laptop after class yesterday."

What could she say?

"If you need help, you tell me."

Mila squeezed her hand. "Thank you."

"Come," Patar called. "The phone is in my house."

Mila hesitated. She was almost certain there were no

landlines on the island. Everything she'd seen since she'd been here had been satellite or Wi-Fi. Which meant he wanted to keep her confined until Agus arrived.

"Hurry, hurry. Agus will be here soon."

That was hopefully also a lie. It should take him at least twenty minutes to get here. "I'm not going inside," she said. "There might be aftershocks."

He waved his hand. "No, no. Earthquake is finished." He grabbed her arm and pulled her towards his house.

Fear prickled her skin. Time to go. Mila jerked her arm away. "It's fine. I'll call when Agus arrives. It's too early at home."

She spotted Dewi across the square. "Dewi!" She hurried over, hearing the man swear behind her. Another ten minutes until she definitely had to leave. But somehow she had to do it without being spotted.

The girl looked up. "Miss Mila!" She wrapped her arms around Mila's waist. "I thought you were dead." The girl burst into tears.

Mila patted her back while searching for some sign of Damien.

She pulled the girl away. "I'm fine, Dewi. You were so brave. I need to speak to someone. You stay here with your family."

Mila moved back over to Ibu Minar and noticed her moped was gone. Damn it. She hesitated. What if Damien had taken it? Maybe she shouldn't point out it was missing.

Two women approached them, one who was perhaps in her mid-forties and the other in her twenties. They shared similar facial features. "Are you the person who saved Ibu?" the older one asked.

Mila nodded.

"Thank you." The woman hugged her. "We were so

worried about her."

"I couldn't leave her behind." She glanced behind her. Patar stood at the edge of the square with a smirk on his face.

Mila forced a smile, her stomach in knots. She had less than ten minutes to get away.

She turned around, searching for a solution, hoping Damien would realise it was her version of the bat signal.

She spotted the little child whom she'd put on the back of her moped before the tsunami had hit. She was being rocked by a woman, perhaps her mother. Mila hurried over. "I'm pleased she is safe."

The woman looked at her in question.

"I put her on the back of the moped with Ibu Minar."

The woman burst into tears. "You saved my baby."

Mila hugged them both and continued to scan the area. She glanced towards the jungle, trying to spot Damien. No luck. If she made a run for it, how far would she get?

"I couldn't find her after the earthquake," the woman sobbed. "My husband forced me to leave because of the tsunami."

"You're both safe now." Mila pulled back, extricating herself from the woman's arms. "I must use the bathroom." That ruse had worked once before.

"The toilet is over behind the houses." The woman pointed.

Relief filled Mila. "Thank you."

She hurried down the side of the nearby longhouse, hearing a shout behind her. She glanced back. Patar was jogging towards her.

Mila ran around the corner of the house and almost ran into Damien. "Keep going," he murmured.

Thank God. She kept running, heading for the toilet

building. When she reached the door, she looked back.

Patar raced into view and Damien grabbed him in a choke hold. In seconds the man was slumped on the ground.

Quickly Damien tied his arms and legs.

Mila jogged back. "He'll yell when he wakes."

Damien nodded. "Let's go before he does." He grabbed her hand and pulled her towards her moped which had keys in the ignition.

"You stole it!"

He grinned. "Yeah. I recognised it was yours and found the keys inside."

He'd been busy while she'd been playing her part.

She jumped on behind Damien and gripped tight.

The acceleration of the bike wasn't great at the best of times, but with two people on it, it was glacial.

As they rode past Patar, he stirred and yelled. A couple of people looked over and frowned.

"Faster!"

"I'm trying."

The engine screamed as Damien opened the throttle and they picked up speed, bumping over the rough dirt ground. They bounced up onto the bitumen and a man darted to his left, heading to a car, while another ran to where Patar was shouting instructions.

Shit.

Fajar's mother pulled Fajar and his sibling into the square right in front of the four-wheel drive. She grinned at Mila as the man honked his horn.

Mila exhaled. It would slow him for a moment.

"The road to the other village is about a kilometre away," she yelled to Damien.

He nodded.

It wouldn't take long for the man to catch up with them and they needed to be off the main road by then.

The small wheels of the bike didn't give them a lot

of grip and the twisty, bumpy road was a death trap.

She clung tighter to Damien and scanned the road ahead of them, searching for the track.

The roar of an engine behind them told her Fajar's family were no longer an obstacle.

"There!" She pointed to the track. It was a significant decline, and she squeezed Damien as he steered the bike down it.

The bumps rattled her brain.

About a hundred metres on Damien swore and abruptly the bike slid to a stop.

Mila leaned to look past. The track had disappeared, falling a few metres straight down and then a path of dirt and debris spilled out from it.

Landslide.

Their escape route was gone.

Chapter 9

Dobby pried his fingers from the moped brakes. They had stopped on the edge of the almost three-metre vertical drop where the land had split.

His heart raced as he scanned what remained of the track. Nothing but a pile of rocks and dirt as far as he could see.

The northern villagers had probably evacuated somewhere below them but above the wave's reach, or taken boats out to sea.

It was far too lumpy for the moped to navigate over carrying the two of them with its small tyres.

They had thirty minutes until evac. He debated going back for the four-wheel drive, but it might not make it down the sharp drop either and he didn't want to risk rolling the vehicle.

They would have to go on foot.

At the roar above him, he whirled to face the main road, as a car raced past without stopping. He waited for the squeal of brakes to indicate they'd been seen but the noise faded into the distance.

He exhaled.

"Can we lift it down?" Mila asked, getting off the

back.

"No point. The tyres won't make it over the dirt." He pushed the bike into the jungle, covering it. "We need to move before the guy from the village realises you're not in front of him. Follow me."

He slid down the slope and then turned ready to catch Mila, but she was right behind him.

"Have you heard from the team? Did Agus leave?"

He smiled. Wasn't that just like her? They'd barely stopped after racing down the mountain and her first thought was of other people's safety. "Yeah. We've got about five minutes before he arrives." He took her hand and set a fast pace down the road. "Good news is, he won't be able to get his car down here either." He scanned her. "Are you all right? I couldn't hear what you were saying, but it didn't look good."

It had been the longest fifteen minutes of his life watching her move through the square, talking to people.

"Agus wanted his man in Desa Agung to bring me to him," Mila explained. "I panicked trying to figure out how to change his mind."

By his estimate they had a couple of kilometres before they reached the northern coastal village. If they didn't make it, there wasn't enough space between the trees to get a ladder down from the helicopter. They needed to hustle.

Dobby glanced up at the road. They were in clear view, so they'd have to hide when they heard another car.

Hopefully Agus would divide his men. He may think they'd hid and doubled back to Desa Agung.

"What did you say?"

"I wanted to marry Vance there."

Though he knew it was a lie, his chest squeezed uncomfortably in an emotion that felt like jealousy.

"Then I asked to call my mother. The old woman who stole my moped offered to lend me her son's phone, and that's when Agus said he would come."

"Quick thinking."

She winced and he noticed the exposed part of her right foot was covered in scratches.

"I should have given you Hawk's boots."

She laughed. "They wouldn't have fit me."

"We could have padded them with two pairs of socks." Stupid of him not to think of it.

"I'm fine." She smiled at him. "Downhill is much easier than uphill. What time is it?"

"Oh seven thirty. We've got half an hour."

She picked up her pace as an engine noise approached.

Damn it. He pulled them into the forest and crouched behind a tree. The road wasn't visible from here which meant Agus shouldn't see them.

"What do we do?"

He pulled Mila down with him. The engine switched off. Voices rose. "Can you understand them?" he whispered.

She nodded. "Agus is swearing. He's telling Ali and another guy to bring the motorbikes."

Dobby closed his eyes. "If the bikes are as new as the cars and they're half decent riders they'll make it down that drop." And that meant there were still people left at the cliff house.

"And he's telling someone else to follow the road."

Damn it.

He keyed his radio. "Radar, there might be two men still at the house. They should leave soon on motorbikes."

"Copy. We'll keep a lookout."

Up ahead the road curved, which would block them from sight but the guy following the road would eventually spot them.

He checked the road.

Correction, two men on foot.

"We need to move as quietly as possible." They had to keep going, otherwise they would miss the extraction.

Mila glanced at the ground.

Dobby followed her gaze to the leaf litter. Luckily everything on the floor was damp and soft and the thick foliage meant they would be swallowed and not visible from the road by the time they were ten metres in. "Follow me."

He kept his steps small so she could step where he stepped and angled away from the road, but still heading towards the village.

"Men leaving the house now," Radar said in his ear.

"What bikes?"

"Brand new dirt bikes."

"Copy." This day kept getting better and better. "We need to pick up the pace."

The ground was uneven, covered in thick tree roots and rocks, but they wouldn't make it to the coast in time for extraction if they didn't hurry.

Her expression hardened. "You set the pace we need. If I can't keep up, I'll tell you."

His admiration for her grew. "Copy."

He set as fast a pace as he dared, watching her, knowing her exhaustion would make her less coordinated, but she fell in beside him. When she tripped, he caught her and encouraged her further, passing her a water flask so she could drink.

He checked his GPS. Another kilometre and they had about ten minutes until extraction. They would make it.

The high buzz of a motorbike engine reached his ears. Still up on the main road, but it wouldn't take them long to reach the village.

He needed a new plan. He crouched and took the canteen from Mila, taking a long sip before giving it back to her. "What's this village like?"

She swallowed, huffing out a breath. "Smaller than the others. It's one long street along the bay with houses on each side. I doubt anything survived." She swiped at the back of her shoulder and her fingers came away red.

"You're bleeding." He shifted to look. New scratches, probably caused by pushing past bushes.

He dug into his pack and handed her his spare shirt. He should have thought of it earlier. "Put this on." Normally he didn't pack extra clothes for a short mission, but it had already been in there when they'd been given the news to go.

The shirt fell to her mid thigh and the darker colour would help her hide better amongst the dark leaves of the jungle and protect her skin from scratches.

His pants would be far too big and more cumbersome than helpful.

He got out his radio. "Radar, do you copy?"

"Copy. Chopper is five minutes out."

He swore. "We need to go one bay west."

"Copy. You going to make it?"

Mila was already getting to her feet even though she was still panting.

"We're going to try really hard to." No promises. That wasn't what she needed right now.

Checking his compass, he pointed in the direction they needed to go. As long as they didn't come across a deep gully, they would be fine.

"You should go on without me," Mila gasped.

He snorted. "No chance in hell. If we miss evac, we'll go with plan... C." He'd lost count of the number of plans he'd been through in the past twenty-four hours.

"Which is?" she asked as she followed him through the undergrowth.

"I'll let you know when I come up with it." He was rewarded by a bark of laughter and he grinned. If she saw humour in his words, she still had more to give. She was tough.

Though Mila's breath was loud and raspy, he picked up the pace, glancing behind him now and then to make sure she was keeping up.

He moved fast but the uneven surface made it difficult to go as quickly as he'd like. Rocks, leaf litter and tree roots meant he had to keep his gaze on the ground half the time rather than watching their surroundings.

Maybe if it hadn't been so rough he would have noticed the change sooner.

The light brightened from the dappled shade of the dense rainforest and he glanced up. About ten metres further was open sky.

And devastation.

The tsunami *had* affected the northern side of the island. In front of them was about three hundred metres of flattened rainforest. It was like a giant had taken a scythe and chopped everything down.

His radio blared. "Evac coming now."

His spirits plummeted.

No way were they getting through it in time.

Massive trees had been felled with branches, vines and roots sticking in the air creating a fence between them and the ocean. It would be a bitch to get through.

And though the sky was clear, there might not be enough space for the helicopter to get a line down without it tangling on the branches.

The ocean was full of debris from the jungle and the town. Likely too dangerous to do an ocean extraction even if they could reach it in time.

But he wasn't a quitter.

He took the lead, using a machete from his pack to cut his way through the branches. Vines tangled around them and it was slow going. Almost a foot of water covered the ground, turning it into shoe-sucking mud.

Everything smelled like a combination of refuse and rot, and sweat trickled down his back from the already humid day.

Mila cried, "Ah!" He turned as her arms flailed and then she fell to the ground with a plop. She grimaced, half her body submerged.

Shit. Dobby offered her a hand.

"My foot is stuck."

He dug the mud away until her foot came free and hauled her to her feet. In the distance he heard the familiar whump whump of a helicopter. They still had a hundred metres until they were in the clear.

It was going to be tight.

Mila's shoes weren't made for this kind of terrain. He shifted his backpack off. "Get on." He crouched with his back to her.

"You don't have—"

"Do it!"

She huffed but jumped on, wrapping her legs around his waist.

His body stirred but he ignored the sensation and grabbed his backpack, charging ahead. The chopper would stop to pick up the others first.

Even as he thought that, the tone of the helicopter changed.

He was confident the helicopter would see them amongst the debris, but there were still too many branches to get an easy lift.

He grunted as he sank almost knee deep in mud and leaf litter. Before he had to ask, Mila climbed off.

Dobby yanked at his leg but the suction was strong.

Fuck this mission.

Mila pulled the leaf litter away, so they could see what they were working with.

The rotor blade tone changed again. Lift off. His radio squawked. "Incoming. Where are you?"

"We're almost there."

The helicopter cleared the hill, but it wouldn't be able to get a line down.

"You've got two bogies incoming," Radar's voice came back. He barely heard him over the noise of the helicopter.

"Tell me." Dobby tugged harder.

"Two motorbikes heading around the bay over all the debris from the village. They're going fast."

Mila dug at the mud around his leg.

"Can you get a line down?" Dobby asked.

"Negative."

The helicopter hovered right above them, close enough for him to see Radar's and Joker's concerned faces as they peered out.

Damn it. He jerked his foot up and finally it popped. He shifted to the edge of the tree line and peered through. The two dirt bikes tore around the point of the bay, maybe two hundred metres away.

"Dobby, there's an Indonesian chopper inbound. Probably carrying aid. They can't see us pick you up."

He bit back the swear words. Dobby gave Radar the sign to go and pulled Mila behind one of the larger tree trunks, forcing her to squat.

The helicopter peeled away as gunshots rang out. Agus's men were firing on it.

"Where are they going?" Mila called into his ear.

"Back to the ship." He exhaled as he considered their options, listening to discern the sound of bike engines from the fading sound of the helicopter. He didn't dare move.

"Are they coming back?"

A great question. In a normal situation he would wait until more rescue workers arrived and then blend in with them until he could get a ride out, but Agus's man had seen him and Agus would have people looking for Mila amongst the aid personnel.

"Damien?" The exhaustion in her voice had him squeezing her hand.

"I'll get us out of here." The helicopter faded and the whine of the motorbike engine grew louder. Best-case scenario Agus's men would assume they'd been picked up by the helicopter before they'd arrived in the bay.

He got his gun ready.

"Damien?" Mila whispered.

"We're going to be fine," he assured her.

Worst-case scenario Agus would have two fewer henchmen.

"Stay quiet and still." He didn't move as the bikes stopped on the shore only a few metres away from them. The engines idled and the two men shouted at each other.

Mila was curled into a ball though her eyes were wide open in fear. He couldn't risk reaching out to her but he gave her what he hoped was a reassuring smile. Maybe she'd reached her limit. She'd been through so much already, but she needed to hold it together until the henchmen left.

The engines revved again and the bikes rode off. Damien waited a few beats before he peered around the tree. Both bikes were heading back around the bay towards the village.

He exhaled. The men weren't well trained. They should have at least searched the area, but maybe they realised they wouldn't win a shoot-out against him.

Either way he was glad. "They're leaving." He moved over to Mila and pulled her into his arms. She clung to him and her body trembled.

He closed his eyes. So close.

They'd been so close to getting off this godforsaken island.

He stroked her hair. "It's all right. We've still got options." Though if an Indonesian helicopter was about to fly overhead, they needed to find cover so it didn't spot them. "Sweetheart, we need to move back into the jungle. Then you can rest."

He pulled her to her feet and then turned so she could climb onto his back again.

This time he took a second to test the ground before putting his weight on it and moved fast, the whump whump of the new helicopter getting closer.

"Are they coming back?" Mila called.

"No. That's not for us."

She tensed and he stroked her thigh to soothe her as he dashed the remaining distance into the dense, undamaged forest. A moment later the helicopter tone changed. It was landing at the northern coastal village the next bay over.

He exhaled and let Mila slide off his back, before he pulled her into his arms again.

"I'm sorry," she sobbed. "Give me a second and I'll stop crying." She waved her hands at her eyes. "It's the exhaustion making me weepy."

He shook his head in disbelief. "If anyone's allowed to cry, it's you, sweetheart." He pressed a kiss to her hair, wishing he could promise her immediate safety. No matter what happened, he was getting her off this island.

Dobby scanned the forest as a matter of habit.

Agus would hopefully think they'd been rescued, but if anyone saw them, they'd report back to him and he and Mila would become hunted again.

But with the Indonesian military on the ground there was hope for Mila.

"We need to get you to the village," Dobby said. "You can tell the Indonesian military who you are, and they'll take care of you."

She brushed the tears from her eyes and sniffed. "What about you?"

He shook his head. "There's no record of me entering Indonesia."

Mila's eyes widened. "Oh." Then she shook her head, her vulnerability of a moment ago disappearing. "I'm not leaving you here when you sacrificed your safety for me."

He scowled. "I'll be fine. I can steal a boat tonight and get away."

"No. We don't know if Agus has any contacts in the military."

"That's a big leap."

"Think about it. Someone outside the island must know what he does, but no one has stopped him. He has to have contacts in the police or military."

It was a stretch. "You're a major-general's daughter. They'd be foolish to risk word getting out."

Her mouth set in a determined line. "It would be easy for them to deny seeing me, and to hand me over to Agus."

There was a very slim possibility she could be right. Could he take that risk?

She stood before him, bedraggled and filthy but with a defiance that made her breathtaking.

He swore. "Fine, but you do exactly what I tell you to do."

Her smile was full of relief. "Of course." She hugged him.

He held her close as he scanned the debris-ridden

ocean. Nothing but trunks, leaves, and parts of houses which had washed around the island.

A boat would be their best bet. Some people may have taken their boats out into deeper water after the earthquake hit in preparation for the tsunami which meant they would still be in one piece.

They were a couple of kilometres away from the bay where the team had first landed, but the zod was no longer there.

The water swirled and pulled and would be a mess of rips and whirlpools for several days at least.

The whole coastline was going to be like this, so swimming to the islet to at least get off the island wasn't an option.

They were both filthy, tired and needed sustenance while he made a plan.

"Let's sit down and eat." He pulled her behind a tree with large roots and pressed her to sit on one of them.

She exhaled. "Thank you. If it wasn't for me you'd be flying to safety right now."

Annoyance made him sharp. "I wasn't leaving without you," he said. "You rescued my whole damn team and that idiot Vance. If it wasn't for you, we would have had a far more difficult extraction." He shook his head, taking in her exhaustion. But it hadn't stopped her pushing to her absolute limit.

"There's no chance in hell I'm leaving you behind."

Chapter 10

The fierce way Damien vowed not to leave her soothed Mila. She worried she was being selfish not going to the Indonesian military. Would he find it easier to escape on his own? But she couldn't in good conscience leave when he'd come after her and given up his chance for an easy extraction.

She rubbed her exhausted eyes. She was wet and filthy, and men with guns were only a short motorbike ride away.

An overwhelming wave of fatigue had tackled her after the team had left and she'd given into the tears.

But for the moments when Damien had held her, she'd felt safe and had been able to rebuild her resolve.

She hoped Vance would endure some kind of punishment for getting them into this mess.

She closed her eyes and leaned into Damien's side, drawing warmth from his body. Not many people would go off script and rescue someone who wasn't part of their mission, but she was really glad he had.

Avoiding Agus by herself would have been almost impossible, and she had no idea how to navigate through the rainforest, but Damien hadn't hesitated once.

"How long have you worked special ops?" she asked.

"A few years." He filled his canteen from water in his pack and handed it to her. "Drink."

The water tasted heavenly and she forced herself not to gulp it down. "What made you join?"

He shrugged. "I wanted to be the best. Only special ops could take me there."

"Why?"

He glanced at her. "Why what?"

"Why did you want to be the best?"

An emotion she couldn't quite read crossed his face. Maybe part bashful, part determination. "I wanted to protect those who were vulnerable. Why did you come here?"

She sighed. "I was running away." She could admit it now after the stress of the past few hours.

He pulled out two sealed packets. "Are you up for a delicious MRE?"

She grimaced. "I've heard they taste disgusting. I'm all right for the moment. I had rice porridge at the village."

He nodded and put one back in his pack. "What were you running from?"

"Life." She picked up a large leaf and tore it into strips. "After the whole thing with Vance blew up in my face, I had to get away." Her smile was sad. "But if we're being honest, I still hadn't figured out what I wanted to do with my life. I've tried so many things, but nothing felt right. I think my family were beginning to find me indecisive and irresponsible."

"There's nothing indecisive about the way you helped those people after the earthquake."

She pressed her lips together. He was right. She shrugged. "Both of my brothers knew what they wanted to do as soon as they'd graduated high school. I've been flitting around trying to find something I felt passionate about." She sighed. "I think it's one reason I fell for Vance's charm."

"The man has charm?" Damien asked.

His incredulity made her laugh. "Yes, he can be very charming when he wants something. He made me feel important and worthy." But Vance had none of Damien's presence and kindness.

"What did he want?"

"Respectability." She placed the strips to the side and picked up a new leaf. "I was a good girl he could date, and my father gave him a job at his company because I vouched for him." She closed her eyes and shook her head. She'd been such a fool.

"Did it work?"

"Yes. We only saw each other a couple of times a week, but when we were together, he wined and dined me, made me feel like I was the centre of his world." She rolled her eyes at her naivety. "He surprised me with a marriage proposal on a day cruise with family and friends and I said yes."

Dobby studied her. "Because you wanted to marry him, or because you didn't want to seem indecisive?"

He knew her well already. "The latter. I wasn't ready for marriage, but I thought maybe we needed to spend more time together. I decided to surprise him by cooking him dinner one night and caught him in bed with another woman."

Damien scowled. "He's more of a fool than I thought if he cheated on you."

His words were a balm. Her confidence had been shaken after that night. "When we broke up, my father fired him. It turns out he wasn't doing any work and the only reason Dad hadn't fired him earlier was he didn't want to upset me." Somehow she'd become the weak one her father felt he needed to protect. Perhaps if he'd confided in her earlier, she might have seen Vance for who he truly was.

"And so you came here?" Damien placed his empty MRE packet back in his backpack.

She nodded. "Mum volunteered here twenty years ago when the last tsunami hit. She kept in touch with a few people and they mentioned they wanted someone to teach their children English. They hoped to increase tourism to the area." She smiled. "I decided to come here without telling anyone but the woman on the island." She sighed. "I should have told my parents. Then Mum would have told me how much Agus hated her."

He handed her another leaf. "Have you enjoyed yourself?"

"Yes." She wove the strips together creating a rope like she'd been taught. "It's such a different life, but the people are so lovely, and I enjoy being connected with nature and the slower pace. I finally felt as if I was doing something meaningful." She scowled. "But I won't ever be able to come back thanks to Vance and Agus."

He stroked her thigh and warmth spread through her body.

"Tell me about Agus. What does he do?"

"From what I can gather he's a smuggler; drugs, cargo, whatever you want. He might also be a pirate, stealing from boats coming through the area."

"Are people scared of him?"

"Some are. As long as you do what you're told and stay out of his way, you're safe." She sighed. "But some see him as a saviour, bringing wealth to the island."

"How did you stay off his radar before Vance came?"

"I had nothing of value and he didn't know who my

parents were. Those who knew kept quiet." The first couple of weeks she'd been a little concerned, but Agus had lost interest when a large group of surfers had arrived.

Damien took a long drink from his canteen and then gestured with it to her legs. "Do you want to use a little to clean up?"

She hesitated. "How much have you got?"

"About nine litres."

She shook her head. "We might need it. I'll go down to the ocean when it's clear and wash."

He nodded and clipped the canteen back to his belt.

"Will Agus give up searching for us?"

"I hope so. The chopper is probably part of the relief effort, or the military taking stock of the damage. Agus will want to talk to whoever's in charge."

She nodded. "So what's plan C?"

He smiled. "A boat's our best bet. We can't keep trekking through the jungle as we are. Your foot will get torn to shreds."

He was right. Her feet already stung with dozens of micro cuts. "Do we need to wait until that chopper leaves?"

"Yeah." He scanned the canopy and seemed satisfied. "I don't want to get caught out in the open when it flies over. They might think we need rescuing."

He spread a dark sheet over the ground between two buttress roots. "Lay down. Get some rest. We've got some time before we need to leave."

"What about you? You haven't slept at all." He had to be exhausted.

"I'm used to it." He grinned. "Special forces, remember? We're the best of the best."

She smiled because he wanted her to, but she touched his arm. "Tell me if you need me to stand guard while you sleep."

His expression changed from surprise, to gratitude, to something deeper. He leaned forward slowly, his eyes on hers and then lightly kissed her lips. "You're killing me," he murmured.

Her heart thumped and she wanted to deepen the kiss, but he pulled back and tapped on the blanket. "Bedtime."

Her heart rate didn't slow as she lay down. Damien wasn't the kind of man she was used to. Her peers at university had been more interested in extra-curricular activities than learning, and the men she met at her parents' social events were all looking to get ahead and if that included seducing the boss's daughter, all the better. Only Vance had fooled her.

She shook the memory away.

Childish or selfish.

There was nothing childish or selfish about Damien.

His confidence and competence as he'd driven the moped down the mountain had been shockingly arousing. And the way he'd handled his gun...

Her cheeks heated.

But she'd seen a softer side to him as well.

His genuine concern for her when they'd first met. His fear when looking for Ethan. The no-nonsense way he cut through Vance's bullshit.

All of it added up to a man she wanted to get to know better.

She trusted him when he said he'd get them out of here. His conviction was impossible to dismiss. And she knew enough about the special forces to understand if he couldn't help her, no one could.

But she was the weak link here. If she couldn't keep up and move when they had to move, she'd get them both killed.

And she couldn't risk Damien like that.

With that in mind she turned her attention to sleep.

***

Dobby exhaled in relief as Mila closed her eyes and almost immediately fell asleep. Every time he thought he understood who she was, she did something that surprised him. Never in all his operations had his target cared about his well-being.

And despite her exhaustion, she was thinking strategically. He shouldn't have offered her the water to clean herself. Not when they might be here for a few more days and would need it all for drinking. He'd been worried about her comfort.

Foolish, losing focus of the mission.

But after a few short hours, he cared for Mila more than he was comfortable with.

He closed his eyes for a second and exhaled again.

What a day.

The radio he used wouldn't be able to contact the helicopter or the ship, and though he had a satellite phone, there was no point using it until he had a plan. For the moment they were on their own.

They had enough food and water for two days, and they could shelter in the forest. But soon the villages, waterways, and skies would be full of emergency response people searching for survivors.

If they were picked up, it would be obvious he was special forces, and he had no legitimate reason to be here.

Finding different clothes would be useful though he doubted anything the villagers owned would fit him even if it had survived.

He definitely wanted to get Mila new shoes.

Maybe something would wash up on the beach. He didn't want to go far into the water with the rips and whirlpools from the tsunami.

What a mess.

Dobby glanced at Mila. Leaving her alone wasn't the best option, but he had to scout the village and the ocean.

The salvage operation would be well underway and if there was a boat to salvage, he wanted it.

The rotors of the helicopter nearby whirled. He checked the canopy covered them as the noise increased.

Mila sat bolt upright with a gasp, eyes wide with terror. He placed a hand on her shoulders. "It's OK. It's the helicopter leaving."

She nodded, but glanced towards the ocean, her eyes a little glassy. The sound was a little similar to the tsunami. No wonder she was terrified. He stroked her arm.

After the military helicopter flew overhead towards Batara, he said, "Go back to sleep. I'm going to scout the area, so don't worry if I'm not here when you wake up."

"Shouldn't I go with you?"

He shook his head. "You'll be safer here and I need you well rested."

Though her face still showed her worry, she nodded.

He couldn't help touching her. "I won't let anything happen to you, sweetheart." He brushed a kiss against her forehead.

She cupped his cheek, her hand soft and warm. Her eyes searched his and she smiled. "I know you won't." She kissed his cheek and then lay down again.

Dobby's breath left him. The faith she had in him was humbling. He waited until she was asleep again and then took his scope and his rifle and moved through the jungle towards the small village.

When he got to the tsunami devastation on this side, he found a high spot and scanned the area. The two motorbikes weren't in sight, but that didn't mean they were gone.

There wasn't a building left standing here. What was left of the wooden structures was pushed against the trees or strewn along the shore. The bay was full of floating items; a soccer ball, fishing nets, furniture.

Some people stood around talking, others crying and comforting each other, and still more had started the inevitable clean up.

Given the choice he would help them, but right now his priority was Mila's safety and that meant getting her off the island.

Slowly he scanned the ocean for anything he could use as a boat.

The bow of a fishing vessel was pointing straight up in the air and as he watched, another fishing boat approached it, tied a tow line and began dragging it to shore. It had only gone a few metres when it became clear it was only the front portion.

He kept searching, stopping when he spotted something that might be useful, before realising it was too broken and moving on.

As he was almost finished his scan, he spotted something dark floating low in the water out in the bay, covered in debris.

No fucking way.

He zoomed closer and followed the sleek lines.

He grinned. The zod.

No one had noticed it yet. Only the one fishing boat was in the bay, sifting its way through the debris for anything to salvage and the zod was still far enough away, about twenty metres offshore. It was impossible to see what condition it was in, but the two motors were still attached and it was almost completely full of water and debris. Enough of the pontoon sections were intact to ensure it hadn't sunk which was a great sign.

The village ended about two hundred metres from

where he was and no one nearby had started cleaning up.

But there was no way he'd be able to pull the zod to shore here without notice and he and Mila would be vulnerable if they swam out and the engine didn't start.

He wasn't sure how strong a swimmer Mila was either.

Best option would be to tow it around the bay to the other side and bring it to shore where he could take his time examining it.

The water swirled still, which would be dangerous, but if he dragged the boat closer to the shore, he'd be able to walk it around the bay.

Should he tell Mila? If something happened to him, she'd be alone, and he'd promised he wouldn't leave her.

Damn.

With another check to make sure no one else had noticed the zod and the fishing vessel was still on the opposite side of the bay, he hurried back to where he'd left Mila.

She lay curled on her side, some of the tension gone from her face. Her legs were covered in mud and her face was covered in scratches and bruises, but she still looked beautiful.

He hesitated, not wanting to disturb her when she finally slept but he didn't want her to think he'd abandoned her if something happened to him in the ocean.

He gently touched her leg. "Mila, sweetheart. Wake up for me."

She blinked at him sleepily and he fought back the temptation to kiss her awake.

"I've found the Zodiac. I'm not sure what condition it's in, but I'm going to swim out to investigate."

She sat up, pushing loose hairs from her face. "Isn't

that dangerous? The water's still too unpredictable."

"It's our best chance, and it's not far from shore. I'll tow it around to this bay. I just wanted to tell you where I was going."

She frowned. "Why? In case you didn't come back?"

He shrugged. "There are risks with everything."

"I'm coming with you." She got to her feet.

"No. I'm a strong swimmer. I need to concentrate on what I'm doing, not worry about you."

"I'll watch from the shore. If you run into trouble, I can rescue you."

"If I run into trouble, you'll only get yourself into trouble by trying to rescue me. There are plenty of things I can grab on to. The worst that will happen is I'll get pulled out to sea."

She glared at him. "Oh good."

Her sarcasm made him smile and he dug into his pack, pulling out some rope. It might be long enough if he needed rescuing. He handed it to her. "You can throw me a line if I'm in trouble, but only if I give you the signal." He waved his hands to demonstrate. "Otherwise I don't want you breaking from the cover of the jungle." He handed her his scope as well. "Use this to keep an eye on what people are doing in the village. If anyone comes near you, hide."

"All right."

The last thing he pulled out was his spare pair of thick socks. "Put these on. They're not as good as shoes, but they'll protect your feet a little."

Quickly she did so and then they moved back to the bay. It took him a moment to spot the zod again. It was perhaps ten metres further out than it had been and it looked as if it was being pulled away from the shore by the current.

Shit.

He jogged through the jungle to where he had the

least amount of open ground to cover. Mila took a moment to catch up. He pointed out the boat to her. "The plan is to swim it around the bay as it is and then check its condition where no one is around."

"What if the current is too strong?"

"Then I'll test the engine or use the oars." Maybe some of the oars would still be with it. "No matter what happens, stay here. I will come back for you. There's enough food and water in the pack for two days."

"Damien, you're scaring me."

"Just coming up with Plan D."

She gave him a shaky smile. "Be careful."

"Always. I have to go before it drifts further out." Dobby took the scope from her to scan the people closest to them, but no one was looking their way. He couldn't delay leaving her any longer.

He gave the scope back and then dashed across the debris-ladened shore to the water, all the while listening for shouts of alarm. At the water he went low, pulling his way across the sand until it was deep enough to swim.

Immediately the water pulled at him, tugging him this way and that.

It was difficult to spot the boat with the rest of the rubbish in the water, but he used breaststroke to part the debris.

The black water smelled like refuse and he refused to think about what might be in it.

The further he got away from the shore, the more the current pulled him out to the ocean. The boat was still about twenty metres away, but it was floating in the same direction.

He increased his pace, as part of a bedroom dresser hit him. He absorbed the weight and pushed past it.

Only ten metres to go.

In the distance he heard the fishing boat coming

closer. He lifted his head over the debris to look. It was heading in his direction, but the captain wasn't looking at him or the boat.

Still it wouldn't be long before he spotted it if it kept coming this way.

Dobby pushed hard as the engine noise dropped to an idle. He exhaled. Hopefully the captain had found something he needed to take back to the shore.

His hands grasped the rope on the side of the boat and he clung on to give himself a second's rest.

Made it.

Now to get it back to Mila.

Chapter 11

Mila tucked herself low amongst the thick ground cover, hidden behind a palm tree. Damien's pack was within easy reach. She ignored the insects crawling over her and the itch from a leaf rubbing against her leg. Her eyes were glued to Damien as he made his way down to the shore.

As he hit the ocean, she glanced towards the village but people were too busy to notice one man rush across the shore and into the filthy water.

Her breath caught in her throat as he breast-stroked towards the flooded inflatable. It seemed much further away now that he was in the ocean and she had some reference of sizes.

She couldn't tear her gaze from him to scan the rest of the bay. Her gut told her if she wasn't watching him, something bad would happen.

A ridiculous superstition, but one she couldn't shake.

His strokes were confident and he seemed unencumbered by his clothes and boots as he made his way closer and closer to the boat. Finally he reached it, ducked around the bow and disappeared from view.

A minute later he reappeared and pulled the boat towards the point.

Mila exhaled and she took a second to scan the village. A man stood on the shore scanning the ocean. He was too far away for her to see clearly, but he was looking towards the boat.

She put the scope to her eye and the young man came into sharp focus. Dressed in a navy-blue T-shirt and black pants, he had once picked up a student from her class. He gestured someone else over and pointed.

Agus's bodyguard, Ali. He must have been on one of the motorbikes.

Which meant the two men with guns were still nearby. Her skin prickled.

Damn. Had they seen the boat?

The fishing boat was hauling a table onboard. The young man on the beach waved and yelled at the captain, pointing towards Damien and the Zodiac.

She glanced back at Damien who was checking the village now and then. Could he see what was happening?

There was no way to warn him. What would he do in this situation? She needed to be calm and wait to see what happened next. Damien was an experienced soldier, and no matter what happened, he would work out what to do.

The fishing boat was slowly making its way back to shore with its hull full and the young man was waiting for it. Damien had some time.

Mila continued scanning, taking in the utter devastation of the village and her heart ached. Where the village had once stood was a rubbish heap of wood, clothes and plastics. They'd lost everything, though women and children were already combing through for items to salvage. Men were clearing building materials, piling up things that were damaged, and those that could be repaired.

Damien wasn't making much progress. He was far enough out that if he swam in her direction, he would make it around the point, but the water was dragging him the other way.

Her heart raced and she impatiently swatted an insect from her neck and pulled up the collar of Damien's shirt. Her scan shifted back to the men on shore where the fishing boat had just arrived. People were unloading a table and other bits of furniture and the men were talking to the captain.

The young man pointed to where the inflatable had been, not where Damien now was. Mila scanned the water where they were pointing and spotted a cupboard floating doors up.

She exhaled. Hopefully that was what they were after.

But Damien was getting further and further out to sea.

Her muscles tightened. What if the boat engine didn't work, and the oars were missing? He might not be able to fight the pull of the ocean and she'd be stuck here, by herself.

She brushed the sweat from her brow and exhaled.

No matter what happened, he would come back for her.

He'd promised.

As she watched, he swam to the ocean side of the craft and pulled off a large piece of wood that was inside the Zodiac. Then he pulled himself into the boat.

It barely moved and stayed low in the water. No one from the shore should have seen him. He kept his body low and pulled the casing from the engine.

Wouldn't the noise attract attention?

Suddenly she spotted movement in her periphery. She scanned her surroundings and spotted Ali and the young man who had been talking to the captain walking along the shore searching the water. Shit. They were a hundred metres away from her, but if she made any movement, she'd attract their attention.

The next nearest tree she could hide behind was three metres behind her, but the ground cover wasn't high. Still, if she was fast, she should make it.

She packed the scope away and lifted the pack, grunting with the effort.

Holy crap what did Damien have in there? It had to be twenty kilos or more.

Carefully she hefted it onto her back and checked where the men were. They were moving fast down the shore but had to watch where they were treading because of all the rubbish, and they were scanning the water more than the forest.

She glanced at the boat but Damien wasn't inside. Her heart clenched. Maybe he'd seen the men and slid into the water.

The murmur of voices switched her attention to her own safety. She checked the men were looking out to sea and shifted from tree to tree, confirming their location before moving to the next one. It wasn't until she moved about ten metres into the jungle that she breathed a little easier.

But not knowing what was happening with Damien made her chest tighten.

And what if the men spotted the boat from here? They might send the fishing boat out to him. Or simply open fire.

If the fishing boat towed the boat to shore, they'd be screwed.

Too many options.

Too many unknowns.

"Maybe it's just the current," a man said in Indonesian.

She froze. They were close.

"It's moving too fast to be the current," Ali said. "We should call Agus."

"And if you're wrong? He'll punish us for making him come here."

Mila crouched down and tucked herself and the pack close to the tree trunk. They'd spotted the Zodiac. She had to do something.

"If I'm right, he'll reward us."

Their voices drew closer. "Didn't you say the English teacher escaped in the helicopter?"

Both men stepped into view through the trees. Ali only had to turn around and he'd spot her. "The boat is proof the men were here."

Her heart raced, and she focused on long, slow, quiet breaths.

She couldn't lift the pack without making a noise, so she left it next to the trunk, covering it with leaves, before inching her way around the other side of the tree. The younger man turned and spotted her, his eyes wide.

Indecision crossed his face.

Hell. Could she outrun them? Not if Ali pulled a gun on her.

So she needed a head start. But if they were busy chasing her...

This was her way to enable Damien to get the boat. Before she considered the implications she gasped and moved, stepping on a twig as she did so.

Ali whirled around and caught her gaze. He smiled.

Yeah, all he was interested in was Agus's good favour. She turned and ran deeper into the jungle, away from the village and the shore, making as much noise as she could.

Where should she run to? She couldn't lead them back to the bay where Damien was headed.

Focus on evasion first. Then she'd figure out how to get back to Damien.

Ali's cry was loud, hopefully loud enough for Damien to hear and realise something was wrong.

Branches and vines scraped her legs and feet, but she didn't slow. She had to get far enough ahead to hide.

Footsteps pounded behind her and she risked a glance back. Ali was gaining on her.

Lungs burning, she pushed herself faster, scanning the forest ahead for a path.

She stepped on a rock, the uneven surface causing her ankle to roll and she stumbled, trying to catch herself before she fell.

Her foot landed hard and pain shot through her ankle. She shrieked and fell to the ground, narrowly missing a plant covered with thorns.

She twisted, trying to get up, but the pain in her ankle was too much.

Ali came to a stop in front of her and smiled. "Mila, Agus will be happy to see you're all right."

Her pulse raced. At least they had stopped looking for Damien.

She had to delay their return to the village for as long as possible.

"I think I broke my ankle."

***

Damien glanced up at the shout in time to see the two men who had been walking along the shore dash into the forest.

Shit. Mila.

Which meant he had to get back to shore.

He'd finished cleaning out one engine casing and reassembling it when he noticed the men on the shore. Three of the oars were still strapped to the inside of the pontoons and the bow was full of fronds and debris, but he didn't clear it yet. It camouflaged the boat and kept it low in the water.

Instead he slipped back into the dirty water and pulled the boat towards the point. The swirl of the water wasn't as strong this far out and it was easier to move.

Dobby kept his eye on the shore and a few minutes after the men had disappeared, they reappeared pulling a limping Mila with them. She didn't have the backpack with her, and she was injured.

The older man, who was one of Agus's men, spoke into a radio, but Dobby couldn't hear anything.

Mila glanced towards him and he lifted a hand to show he'd seen her. She averted her gaze with a slight nod.

Good. She understood he would come for her.

Now he needed to know what they would do with her—take her back to Agus's house, or keep her here.

He wished he had his scope with him. He would have to find it before going after her.

Agus's man sat Mila down on a tree trunk at the edge of the village.

Dobby kicked harder, making it around the point and into the next bay. He brought the boat closer to the shore until his feet touched and then he dragged it through the water until he found a spot to hide it.

As he was about to empty all the rubbish from the inside, he heard an engine out to sea.

Damn. He pushed the boat deeper, so it blended with the rest of the debris and crouched down.

A luxury cruiser motored around the point coming from the main village. He spotted a man on board who he would almost guarantee was Agus.

Going to pick up Mila.

He kept low in the water until the boat passed the

bay and then moved fast, dragging the boat up the shore and pulling the bung from it to drain the water. While it drained, he moved debris around the boat to hide it. It was far too heavy for him to pull it up the crowded beach. He tucked the bung in his pocket and ran into the jungle, heading for the other bay.

Thankfully only a couple of hundred metres separated them and as he reached the other side he spotted the luxury cruiser anchored, while a tender made its way to the shore. Mila still sat on the trunk.

Dobby took his bearings to figure out where he'd left her. His backpack would have to be close along with his rifle. Cautiously he moved through the edge of the forest until he noticed broken branches.

He spotted a compressed area and grinned, shifting away the leaves to expose his equipment.

The inflatable reached the shore. There were only three men; the captain, Agus's man, and the younger man. He could shoot them all, but the Indonesian military might have left people on the ground here and he didn't want to enter a firefight.

It was unclear what Agus would do to Mila. He might be satisfied with money which he wouldn't get if Mila was dead.

But would he punish her for running or for what her mother had done all those years ago?

Dobby kept his gun trained on them as she limped down to the water. If she could put weight on her ankle, it wasn't broken, but it would make escape more difficult.

He shifted his pack on his back as the tender made its way back to the luxury cruiser.

His muscles tightened when Mila boarded the cruiser and the man on board greeted her. They moved below deck.

Dobby waited only long enough to make sure the

cruiser was heading back towards the main village before he returned to the bay where he'd left the zod.

He replaced the bung now the water was well drained but didn't remove the camouflage yet.

As the cruiser moved into view, he crouched down behind the boat and pulled out his scope. One man on the bow giving directions through the debris, one at the helm, and another two at the back of the boat. No sign of Mila or Agus.

His options depended on where they took Mila. They could keep her on the boat, or take her back to Agus's place.

With no team to back him up, he had to rely on stealth tactics.

But one advantage was the debris forced the cruiser to crawl through the water. When it went around the point, Dobby risked testing one engine. It coughed on his first attempt, but purred to life on the second one.

He grinned, revving it lightly and then pushed the zod off the shore. He wanted to get as close to the main village as possible. He motored slowly across the bay, still keeping low against the pontoons.

More search boats would be coming into the area and he couldn't be spotted. As he reached the point, Agus's cruiser was heading past the next bay. He waited until it was gone and then moved around the point. He recognised the rock formations. This was the bay they'd landed in less than twelve hours ago.

Batara was the next bay around. He'd have to go by foot to avoid being seen.

He drove onto the shore avoiding the sharper looking rubbish and tied the zod to a large trunk.

He could only hope the villagers had enough to do in Batara and wouldn't start searching the other beaches for things they could salvage.

He covered the zod and then headed towards

Batara.

To rescue Mila.

Chapter 12

Mila's ankle was definitely sprained. It hurt when she stepped, but at least she didn't need to lean on anyone to walk. She gratefully sank onto a large tree trunk on the shore to wait, with Ali and the young man standing guard. Not that they needed to. She wouldn't be able to run from them now.

"Where is the soldier?" Ali demanded.

Mila sighed. He'd asked her the question multiple times on the walk here. "I told you. He escaped in the helicopter."

"Why didn't they take you?"

"I wasn't their mission, Vance was. I stayed to help here."

"Then why were you hiding in the jungle?"

"I wasn't hiding, I was coming to the village, but I must have got a little turned around." She gave a helpless shrug. "It's hard to walk in a straight line in the jungle."

"Why run from me then?" Ali asked.

"Because you stole my laptop and do whatever Agus tells you to. I didn't want Agus to know I was still here so I could help people without him bothering me." It would have been the truth if Damien had left her here.

Ali grunted a non-committal sound.

She casually scanned the ocean, trying not to make it obvious she was looking for Damien. Relief swept through her when he raised his hand in acknowledgement.

He would come for her.

Five minutes later, Agus's luxury cruiser motored into the bay. Of course. With the road damaged, this was the only way to get around the island.

It mustn't have spotted Damien because she was certain Agus would have stopped and there hadn't been enough time.

A small tender was lowered from the cruiser and motored into the bay. Agus wasn't on board.

Getting his minions to do his dirty work.

Would Damien rescue her before the boat got to the shore?

She fought the urge to look behind her, not wanting to tip off the others that he was still here.

The tender reached the shore, and she limped over, hissing at the pain in her ankle.

As they motored out, she stared at the shoreline where she'd waited for Damien. She'd hoped he would reach her before the cruiser arrived, but he hadn't.

He was probably working on Plan E. The thought made her smile.

"You're happy to see Agus?" Ali asked.

She turned her attention to the luxury cruiser where Agus was standing on the deck. Today he wore a red polo shirt and beige slacks and appeared as if he'd had an excellent night's sleep. His wide smile wasn't at all comforting.

Mila on the other hand was covered in mud and scratches and fatigue weighed heavily in her head.

She exhaled. She could do this. The villagers had

only seen her with Damien before the extraction.

One man on the cruiser grabbed the tender's rope and held it steady while Ali helped her off. She winced as pain shot through her ankle and awkwardly hopped her way up the steps to the main deck.

"Mila, you are injured?" Agus stopped a metre away from her and curled his lip as he took in her filthy appearance.

"I sprained my ankle." She was tempted to brush off some of the dried mud from her legs onto his pristine white deck, but it would be better if she let him believe she was more subservient after her ordeal.

"Perhaps you shouldn't have run from Ali."

"He scared me." She took in a shuddery breath. "It's been a hellish few hours. After the earthquake I was caught in the tsunami and almost died. Then Vance and the special forces men used me to escape, without taking me with them."

Agus shook his head as he gestured for her to follow him. "I'll protect you. Come. I have first aid downstairs. You can shower and I'll find you some more clothes to wear."

She glanced back to the island but still couldn't see Damien. Would Agus lock her below deck? "Where are we going?"

"Back to the village. The doctor has reopened the medical centre. We can get your ankle seen to and then you can rest at my house."

Rest. Right.

"Take your socks off here and then Ali will help you downstairs." Agus waved his hand, not wanting to touch her, and headed below deck.

Nerves prickled her skin as she peeled off the socks and shoes and placed them on the clean, white deck. Ali handed her a bowl to wash her feet in and then a towel to dry them.

A bruise had already formed on her sprained ankle and she touched it gingerly. It didn't feel broken.

Ali threw her socks and shoes into a nearby bin and she bit her lip to stop from protesting. Maybe she wouldn't need them if Damien rescued her from the boat. Mila took Ali's arm and hop-limped down the stairs to a beautiful lounge area. Agus sat on a sofa that followed the curve of the boat, his arms stretched out along the back rest. "I put some of my sister's clothes in the bathroom. You should shower."

He didn't want her dirtying his boat.

The idea of getting clean was enticing, but was it safe? "Is there a lock on the door?"

Agus inclined his head. "Naturally, but if you take too long, I do have a key."

She forced a smile. "A shower sounds lovely." She could clean her new cuts and scratches and examine her ankle.

Ali led her down a corridor to a bright white and gold bathroom which contained a large basin, toilet, and a self-contained shower cubicle. Thick white towels were folded underneath the bench and on top was a beautiful blue summer dress with strappy sleeves and some underwear.

Much better than what she was wearing now, if it fit, but not the best outfit for a daring escape.

The bathroom had no window. The only exit was the door she'd come through.

"Don't be long," Ali said.

Mila locked the door behind him and while the lock snicked into place, it wouldn't be hard to pick it, or force it open.

She stared at herself in the mirror, barely recognising the wretch in front of her. Mud and dirt covered her, as did dried blood from the scratches. Her ponytail was barely hanging in there and exhaustion made her eyes shadowed.

She exhaled. She was alive, and she'd be thankful for that. After she was clean, she'd work on an escape plan. She washed her hands and picked up the dress, measuring it against her body. It should fit.

She stripped off her bag. If she had time, she'd wash it, but it wasn't her priority. She ran the shower, not waiting until it warmed before she stepped under the spray fully clothed.

The water was blissfully clean, and she scrubbed at her face and limbs, getting most of the dirt off her before she reached for the shampoo bottle and lathered her hair in soap.

She glanced towards the door as she rinsed herself.

She would have to get naked eventually if she was putting on dry clothes. She stripped off Damien's shirt, her thin top and shorts, washing any remaining dirt from her skin and stepped out of the shower, leaving the water running.

Fastest shower on record.

She placed her wet clothes in the sink and dried herself, before putting on the dress and underpants Agus had left for her. She'd missed a bit of dirt on the underside of her arm near her elbow and she scrubbed it off.

Mila wrapped her hair in the towel and then turned her attention to the bag she'd had slung over her body since the earthquake.

She emptied out the contents; purse, comb, hand sanitiser, tissues which were a sodden mess, a couple of bandages she'd grabbed from the medical centre, and the multi-tool.

It felt like an age ago that she'd used it to cut the vines from the door.

Flicking it open, she rinsed the dirt from it and checked the knife. She had a weapon.

Pity she didn't have any pockets to put it in.

The bandages caught her eye and she grinned, unwrapping one quickly and then wrapping it firmly around her breasts. It would make a decent makeshift bra and she could tuck the multi-tool into her cleavage. Perfect.

With a glance at the door, she rinsed her clothes, the bag and its contents and then turned off the shower as someone banged on the door.

"I won't be long," Mila called.

She squeezed water from her wet clothes and folded them small, placing them with Dobby's shirt and then wrapping the lot in a large hand towel which she placed into her damp bag. She threw the sodden tissues out and used the comb to remove the knots from her hair and tie it back into a ponytail and then checked the drawers and cupboards for anything useful.

A brand new toothbrush and toothpaste, plus some tissues.

"You've got one minute," Ali called.

"Just brushing my teeth." She gave into the temptation and cleaned her teeth and then studied herself in the mirror.

Dark circles under her eyes and myriad cuts over her arms. Her hand went to the waterproof bandage on her arm where Axle had stitched her gash. If Agus asked about the injury, she'd say she'd got it the evening before the earthquake.

Her legs were worse than her arms from all the running through the jungle, but nothing looked red and inflamed yet.

Another bang on the door had her jumping. She exhaled and looped her bag over her head before limping over to the door and pulling it open. She smiled at Ali. "Sorry. There was a lot of dirt to scrub off."

He held out his arm to help her walk.

"How did your family fare. Did they escape the tsunami?"

He grunted. "Most were in the mountains for a wedding."

Mila's eyes widened. "Are you related to Dewi?"

He nodded.

"She was pretty scared when her grandmother was stuck."

He squeezed her arm. "Did you save them?"

"Yes. Fajar's family and Ibu Minar needed help as well. They got away." She needed his goodwill even if she knew he wouldn't betray Agus.

His lips pressed together, and he pulled her into the living room where Agus waited.

"Ah, don't you look nice now." He gestured to a seat across from him. "Please help yourself to refreshments."

On the coffee table was a bottle of water and fresh fruit. Mila glanced out the window to see they were coming into the bay at Batara and then lowered herself to the seat. "Thank you." She cracked the seal on the bottled water and drank half of it.

Then she ate an already peeled rambutan.

"Tell me what happened to Vance," Agus said.

Mila placed the seed on a plate. "He escaped in the helicopter which came to the island, the one Ali saw."

"You were seen leaving Desa Agung with a special ops soldier. Where is he? What was he doing here?"

She closed her eyes. "They were here for Vance. They approached me in Batara after the earthquake asking where he was. I told them he was staying with you." She shrugged. "I was too busy helping villagers to worry what kind of mess Vance had got himself into."

"He's a foolish man."

Mila raised her bottle. "I'll drink to that."

"What happened after the tsunami hit?" Agus asked.

The strength of a good lie was to tell the truth whenever possible. "I saw the special ops men escaping in a black car just before the wave hit, but one of their men fell out of the car. He and I were swept up by the wave." She shuddered and rubbed at her hot skin. "When the wave subsided, I found him in the jungle and his team came to pick him up. He was injured badly, and they needed my knowledge of the island. They promised to take me with them when they left."

"It was you at the medical centre." Each comment was calm and measured with an almost knowing edge to it.

"Yes. We took a stretcher and some meds."

"Why not leave immediately?"

If she mentioned the Zodiac would he get his men to search for it? "Their evacuation was supposed to be on the beach. With the tsunami waves it was too dangerous so they had to wait for the all-clear."

"Why did you go to Desa Agung?"

"With their injured soldier, they needed the helicopter to land and the only place was your cliff."

Agus scowled. "So you were the distraction?"

She nodded. Here she had to be careful with what she said. He hadn't mentioned her mother yet. "They thought you would be interested in me for some reason." She shrugged. "I told them you only wanted me to help Vance and if Vance was gone, you wouldn't be interested any longer. They didn't agree." She laughed as if it was ridiculous.

"What about the soldier with you?"

She frowned. "He said he was there to protect me and would take me to the extraction point." She ate another rambutan. "I figured they were paid to see threats everywhere, but then Patar was acting weird and I was scared maybe they were right, so I went with the soldier."

"So how are you still here?"

Mila pouted. "Your men chased us and he forced me through the jungle. When the helicopter arrived, the soldier climbed up the rope saying he'd send down a ladder, but then they flew away."

"So they left you here?" Agus said.

She nodded.

"Why were you hiding in the jungle?"

"I wasn't. I was trying to make my way to the village but I got lost."

"Why did you run?"

"Because Ali had a gun and was talking about me. It scared me." She hugged herself and rocked a little. "It's been a hell of a day."

Agus studied her. "Will the soldiers be back for you?"

She shook her head. "I wasn't their mission. They used me just like Vance had." She paused, taking a breath, not finding it difficult to bring tears to her eyes. Fatigue had her emotions close to the surface. "It seems I can't trust anyone's word these days." She exhaled and forced a smile. "Besides, there's far too much work here for me to leave. People need my help." She glanced out the window. "I can't believe how much stuff is floating in the water."

"You need rest and to have your ankle examined by a doctor. You will come to my house." The engines went into neutral and the boat stopped. "Ali will help you back to the tender."

This benevolent Agus gave her goosebumps but she played along. "Thank you."

He still hadn't mentioned her mother. Maybe he hoped she'd forgotten he knew her and wanted her nice and compliant until they got to his house.

Could she come up with an excuse to stay in Batara? She couldn't help much with a twisted ankle, and if she truly trusted him, she wouldn't make up an excuse.

Hopefully Damien would get to her on the transfer between the boat and house.

And if he didn't, he'd already proven he could rescue someone from the house.

Though he didn't have his full team, and Agus might be more vigilant if he didn't believe her.

Maybe Mila would have to rescue herself.

***

Damien found a place on the rocky point where he could watch Batara. In the bright light of day the destruction looked even worse. People were hard at work clearing rubble and several boats were searching the water for things to salvage. About five hundred metres from the shore was the small islet they'd rowed past last night. This side had a cliff face, but the other side might have a beach. That would at least get them off the island.

Across the other side of the bay stood Agus's house in all its glory. From here it appeared as if the tsunami hadn't damaged it.

The luxury cruiser anchored offshore where the rubbish wasn't so thick and Mila and four men boarded the tender and headed into town.

Mila wore a clean, blue dress and her arms and legs were free of dirt. They must have let her shower. She didn't look scared, but she scanned the shore. He didn't dare signal her in case someone else saw the flash of light.

When the tender pulled up on the shore, one man helped Mila off and then supported her as she limped towards the medical centre which had a line of people out the door.

At least they were getting her help.

As he watched, the well-dressed man with Mila

walked to the head of the queue and inside and the rest of them followed. Definitely Agus.

Four men against him and Mila. He had to wait until they were out of the village, away from the Indonesian military who were handing out supplies to people.

Any gunshot would attract their attention and bring them running.

Less than half an hour later, Mila walked out of the medical centre with her ankle strapped and a pair of crutches under her arms.

She wore sandals.

From the medical centre they moved over to another black four-wheel drive and got in. Agus went over to the military men as they were packing up and shook a man's hand.

Perhaps Mila had been right not to go to them for help.

As Dobby suspected, they drove up to the clifftop house, but he couldn't see anything else from here.

He shifted back and considered his options, while the military helicopter took off.

With Mila unable to run, he needed transport. He didn't have Axle's car key decoder and Agus probably wouldn't leave his car out like he had before.

A moped was too slow, but if one of the dirt bikes was there, it might come in handy.

Though he still needed to get from a road to the zod.

He eyed the cliffs.

They'd brought equipment for scaling the cliff in case it was needed and he had the extra harness in his pack which they would have used with Vance.

If he could get the boat to the bottom of the cliff, find somewhere safe to tie it, scale the cliff, find Mila and abseil back down, all without being spotted in the bright light of the day, they had a chance.

He shook his head. That was a lot of ifs.

The zod's engine would attract attention and there were too many boats in the waters for him to escape notice.

Taking the zod the long way around the island would waste fuel he might need, and he still might run into one of Agus's men.

What had Mila told Agus? Did he know Dobby was still on the island?

No. His gut told him she'd have made some kind of excuse, which meant Agus wouldn't be expecting an immediate rescue.

That could work to his advantage.

He moved back into the jungle, making his way around the village towards Agus's house. He needed to get eyes on Mila and search for other transport options. On his way there, he made sure he had more jerky for the dogs.

He made his way up the hill, spotting a few cut vines and debris being shifted to form a path where his team must have come through. The jungle grew to the edge of the cliff top, which was a huge flat rocky area. He stood behind a tree on the edge and scanned the house from bottom to top.

The man who had helped Mila into the clinic was in the ground floor office and the two other men who'd been with the group were patrolling the grounds, each with a dog. In this light he saw how skinny both animals were.

Shame he couldn't rescue them as well.

On the second floor he spotted children playing in a room and on the third floor Agus appeared at a window and looked down at the garden.

Dobby shifted further behind the tree so he wasn't seen. Was Mila in the room with him?

Agus moved away from the window and Dobby

couldn't see anyone else in the room, but he had a shitty angle on it.

Quickly he got the grappling hook from his pack and used it to hook over the lowest branch and haul himself up. From there he could see straight into the room where Mila was tied to a chair.

As he watched, Agus backhanded her and her head snapped back. Dobby swung his rifle up and aimed, but didn't take the shot yet.

The bang would bring all the guards running and he wanted to avoid a firefight, particularly as there were more innocents in the house this time around.

He hadn't brought a sniper rifle because they'd been packing light and Axle was the team's main sniper.

But even if he hit Agus, he still needed to get into the house, cut Mila's ties and get them out without raising an alarm.

All in the middle of the day when anyone glancing out the window would see him dash across the open clifftop to the gardens.

He needed a plan, fast.

***

Just as Mila had suspected, all traces of kindness had evaporated the moment Agus showed her into the guest bedroom. He shoved her into a chair. "Tie her up," he ordered Ali.

Ali hesitated.

"I can easily find a new bodyguard if you're not up for the job," Agus said.

Ali winced and was almost apologetic as he cable-tied her hands behind her and her feet together. She winced at the pull on her muscles, still sore from the tsunami.

She gave silent thanks to Jared who'd insisted on teaching her how to get out of cable tie restraints and hand cuffs one day when he was showing off what he'd learnt at training.

She just had to wait for the right moment.

"Leave us," Agus said.

In seconds, she was alone with Agus. The room was luxurious with a king-sized bed covered in lush pillows, a set of bedside drawers as well as a tallboy on the other side of the room by the door.

It would be a lovely place to stay under different circumstances, but nothing stood out as a potential weapon if she managed to get free.

She turned her attention back to Agus. Others might think him calm, but Mila knew better. The slow walk to the window and back was more of a prowl, his hands twitched minutely as if wanting to punch something, and his eyes were full of malice.

She exhaled, watching him carefully. This was a man she'd never seen before. This was a man who had done things that required guard dogs and bodyguards.

"You were wise not to tell me who your mother was," Agus said.

She didn't respond.

"Do you know what she did to me?"

Mila shook her head, wanting to hear his version of events. Then maybe she could build an argument that wouldn't end with her being killed.

"She arrested me for theft," Agus said, coming to a stop in front of her chair. "I took food for my siblings. My parents died in the tsunami and we had nothing, not even a roof over our heads. We needed to eat."

She didn't ask why it was that her mother had caught him selling the food back to desperate villagers who were starving.

"My arrest left my siblings with no one to look after them. Two died when I was in prison. My engagement was called off and I lost the woman I loved." He smiled. "But in prison I learned how to take control of my life. I came out a better man, one who could take care of his family." He watched her, waiting for a response.

"I'm glad you benefited from it."

His backhand took her by surprise and her head snapped back. She closed her eyes at the pain and let herself go limp, faking unconsciousness.

"Mila." He slapped her cheek roughly, but she didn't respond.

He swore. "Weak woman."

She waited, head hanging, feeling incredibly vulnerable not being able to see where he was. Would he leave, or wait until she came around?

His footsteps moved to the door and then the door slammed closed. Mila waited another minute before she cautiously opened one eye. Slowly she looked around. The room was empty.

Quickly she stood and shuffled away from the chair, glad Ali hadn't actually tied her to it. She squatted fast with her heels out as far as they would go to break the tie around her feet and then slammed her wrists against her back in a downward motion which snapped the ties around them. She rubbed the pain in her wrists as she limped across to the door. Her sprained ankle would make it difficult to run fast enough to outrun Agus, and he had a gun.

She tried the door handle.

Locked.

What were her options?

She went across to the window and peered down three storeys. The multi-tool between her breasts dug into her and she grinned. Quickly she checked the bed had sheets on it and then turned her attention to the heavy wooden tallboy. It took all her effort to push it across the doorway to stop Agus from entering easily.

Next she took her singlet from her bag and hung it over the window sill so Damien would know which room she was in when he arrived.

Then she dragged the sheets from the bed, got her multi-tool out and started cutting strips of fabric.

Chapter 13

Dobby watched in amazement as Mila broke out of her restraints and blocked the entrance to the bedroom with a tallboy. She came to the window, leaning out to check what was below and then placed her singlet on the windowsill. He smiled. Letting him know where she was. He tried to use his scope to flash her, but the tree provided too much shade.

What was her plan? She'd blocked the doorway, so the only other exit was the window.

He couldn't see her anymore and he waited, debating whether he should get closer so he was in position to act, or whether he should stay where he was so he could see into the room.

It wouldn't take much for Agus to break down the door and from here Dobby could shoot anyone coming through.

A motorbike roared up to the house and a man got off and jogged inside. Dobby smiled.

Transport.

He scanned the downstairs rooms and saw Agus and two men in the ground floor office. Agus was waving his hands about, clearly angry.

Dobby wanted Mila away from that room before Agus returned.

Which meant he needed to move.

He gave the grounds one last scan. The guards were at the front of the house. Agus was leaving the office with a jug and the man who'd been on the motorbike was with him. The third man hesitated before following them.

Shit.

He checked Mila's window in time to see her appear there with a handful of white fabric.

She spotted the guards and moved backwards away from the window. A loud banging caused her to whip her head towards the door.

Agus had discovered she'd locked herself in.

More thumps that Dobby could hear from where he sat and the two guards ran inside.

Mila returned to the window, saw it was clear and dumped the handful of fabric out the window. It cascaded down the wall in a braided rope to about a metre from the ground.

She had to be shitting him. She was using bed sheets to climb down?

He wanted to laugh, but he was more concerned about what she'd anchored the sheets to. Would it hold her weight?

As she climbed out the window, the pounding intensified. Damien wanted to go to Mila, but he could cover her better from where he was. At this moment all hostiles were inside and Mila's only danger was falling.

He scanned the room below her. It looked as if it was a lounge room, but it was empty.

She tugged on her rope and started climbing out the window.

The woman was incredible.

Dobby prayed the rope would hold, and she'd have

enough arm strength to lower herself down.

When she passed the second storey window, he slid down the tree and ran across to the motorbike, keeping his gaze roaming for hostiles.

An almighty crack at the room Mila had just vacated and he paused next to the motorbike as Agus's head appeared at the window. His arm moved, gun in hand and Dobby raised his rifle and shot. Blood spurted from Agus's shoulder and he stumbled out of view.

Mila was on the ground and limping towards him. He kickstarted the bike and sped over to her, half an eye on the window above, but no one else appeared in it.

He slid the bike to a stop next to Mila and she jumped on.

There was a shout from above but he didn't turn. He accelerated towards the jungle, keeping low against the handlebars.

Gunshots rang out and Mila squeezed him tighter as he bumped into the jungle and followed the path he'd taken to get here.

As much as he would have preferred to take the road, he didn't want people to see them.

It would raise too many questions.

He slowed out of necessity as he bounced over roots, but the bike's suspension was state-of-the art and handled it with ease.

He couldn't take his eyes off his path to glance behind as he tore through the jungle, the village not far to his left.

Mila relaxed against him, holding tightly, but not stiffly, moving with the bike.

They burst out of the trees, crossed the road that led up the mountain and back into the jungle again.

Not far now until they'd reach the beach where he'd left the zod. He bounced over a high root and Mila shrieked, her weight lifting from the seat behind him. They landed with a thud, the shocks absorbing the impact, but Dobby waited for Mila to settle again before accelerating. In the distance he heard dogs barking.

Damn it.

Not far now. He couldn't go fast through the bumpy terrain and those dogs were quick.

A hundred metres, fifty, twenty, ten.

He braked and Mila was already climbing off, keeping her weight off her sprained ankle. Dobby dumped the bike and carried her to the boat.

He ripped the leaves and camouflage from it, and released the rope as Mila threw the backpack inside.

"Does it work?" Mila asked.

"Yes." He pushed it down the shore into the water and then turned to help Mila into it.

She was already at his side, her face pale, skin clammy.

"Get in." He held the boat steady as the dogs burst out of the jungle onto the beach. He pushed the boat deeper and leapt inside as Mila scrambled to the back and started the engine, shoving it into reverse.

He shifted his rifle into position, monitoring the dogs and jungle as Mila grabbed an oar and used it to move debris out of the way behind them.

One dog stopped at the water's edge barking frantically, while the other plunged straight into the murky water and swam towards them.

It was the same dog as at the medical centre.

Shit. Maybe it would get tired and turn around. There was too much rubbish in the water and the currents were unpredictable.

Mila turned the boat so it was pointing out to sea and the dog kept coming, only a few metres from them. Dobby saw her worried gaze.

They couldn't save the dog. It might attack them.

The dog yelped as a heavy tree trunk bumped into it and its head went under the water.

Mila gasped and stretched her oar out to it. It surfaced, splashing, and latched onto the oar with its teeth.

Dobby swore as she pulled the dog towards the boat. The jungle was still clear and the other dog stood on the shore. "Mila, we can't..." His words died as both she and the dog looked at him with wide imploring eyes.

He swore again. "If it attacks us, it's going back into the water."

She nodded and he swung his rifle around and hauled the dog into the front of the boat, keeping between it and Mila. "Take us out of the bay."

He readied his gun as the dog lay panting in the bow and then vomited sea water all over the boat. Dobby shook his head as Mila laughed and accelerated.

"I've got half a mind to send you to the front to clear debris," Dobby said. He eyed the dog who had finished retching and then shook itself, the water spraying all over Dobby. Then it wagged its tail and lay down, avoiding the vomit which had slid to the middle of the boat.

Well damn.

"I think she likes us," Mila said.

It certainly looked that way. He checked the jungle and then shifted his pack so it stayed out of the vomit. He approached the dog who was watching him with cautious eyes now. Staying low, he reached his hand out and let the dog sniff him and then stroked its chest. Its bones could be seen sticking out beneath its fur.

It really had been starved.

The dog wagged its tail again, this time a little hesitantly.

"You're all right," Dobby said. "You're safe now."

He sighed.

What the hell was he going to do with a dog?

Chapter 14

Mila had nothing left. She'd slumped at the back, hand gripping the rudder, staring out at the ocean as if it was her saviour.

They were almost somewhere they could rest, but he wanted to keep her alert.

"Who taught you how to use these engines?" He'd been impressed that she hadn't even hesitated.

She glanced at him and forced a smile. "My dad. His company builds these. It's how he and Mum met."

"Nice." He kept his surprise to himself. Her father must be worth a lot of money. The whole military used these types of engines because of their reliability. "Keep the speed low. We don't want to damage the boat on any debris."

She nodded.

If he'd had his team with him, he would have rowed, but he couldn't make Mila do more than necessary.

As they cleared the point of the bay, he shifted past the dog to the bow and retrieved an oar to push debris out of their path.

No one had followed the dogs yet, but that didn't mean they were clear. Agus had his boat.

The gunshot wound probably wasn't fatal and Agus could go to the medical centre for treatment. It would keep him busy for a while.

He shook his head, unable to believe everything that had happened since he arrived. Up ahead was the islet where he hoped to rest. It was about five hundred metres offshore and he could walk around it in an hour, but it was uninhabited and that's what he needed.

The unknowns were how shallow the reef was, what kind of state the shore would be in, and whether someone would spot them. There was still no word from the team, but they should have arrived back at the ship by now.

The debris was thinning out so he shifted to the stern next to Mila.

He placed a hand around her shoulders. "I've got this. Why don't you rest up front?"

She leaned into him for a second and then nodded. "Is Trixie OK?"

He frowned and she nodded to the dog. "You've already named her?" That wasn't good.

She smiled. "She looks like a Trixie, don't you think?"

He was not getting caught in that conversation. "If you say so. Watch your step around the vomit."

Mila grimaced and kissed his cheek. "Thank you for letting me save her."

He couldn't refuse after everything she'd been through, but he'd have to drop the dog somewhere. The islet wouldn't be able to sustain her.

He nodded and waited until she shifted up the front and settled next to the dog with her arm around it, before he accelerated again.

The dog snuggled into her. It knew a good person when it found one.

Dobby sighed. So did he. He wanted to get to know

Mila better, but would she want anything to do with him after they returned home? He might remind her too much of this traumatic time, or she might not be interested despite the kisses they'd shared.

Hell, he didn't even know where she lived.

That was a problem for another day. Right now there was a boat at nine o'clock heading towards the island.

He put their boat into neutral while he fetched his scope. Mila glanced at him. "What's wrong?"

"Just checking out who that is." He pointed to the trawler-sized boat making its way through the debris, similar to them.

Mila squinted. "It might be the barge that brings supplies to the island."

Hopefully it wouldn't notice them. They should be far enough away to blend in with the surrounding flotsam and jetsam.

Because if whoever was onboard mentioned them to Agus, it became a whole new ballgame.

They'd have to keep moving rather than hide.

Dobby kept the boat in neutral, not wanting the forward motion to be something people on the boat noticed. He shifted lower as he scanned who was onboard.

The captain was on the top deck behind the wheel, his attention focused on the water in front of him. Another man, probably the first mate, was on the bow directing him, similar to the way Dobby had helped Mila.

A number of crew were on the main deck staring and pointing at the surrounding devastation.

Mila shifted low as well so only the dark pontoons of the boat were visible.

They should blend with the ocean and rubbish.

His hands clenched. He'd given up expecting things

would go the way he wanted on this mission.

There was no reason for the boat to come over here even if the Zodiac was spotted. They had a delivery to make.

That was a good point. They might go on to the next island after the delivery was complete and Dobby wanted to be out of sight by then.

He moved the boat into drive and slowly crept them closer to the island. Mila moved to the bow, her body low as she gave him directions.

Dobby kept monitoring the barge but as they neared the island, the people on the deck moved to the bow to stare at the island in front of them. He increased the speed. They had about another hundred metres before they would be clear of the bulk of the rubbish.

Trees, leaves and coral combined in a treacherous mess on the surface. The occasional dead fish or bird also floated by, but thankfully no humans.

This side of the island had no beach to land on. High black volcanic rocks covered in trees soared above.

He skirted the island, wishing he had a depth sounder. "Watch for the reef," he called.

Mila gave him a thumbs up as they came around the northern side of the islet.

With the barge now out of sight, Dobby relaxed a little. He slowed and scanned the shoreline.

The tsunami had devastated this island as well. Trees were flattened and what had been a sandy shore was covered in logs and branches. It would be difficult to pull the boat onto the shore, particularly with only two of them.

He called out to Mila, "I'm going around the western side."

She nodded.

The sun beat down, heating the black rubber of the

Zodiac, radiating it back at them. Sweat dripped down his back.

Mila wore only her strappy dress and would get burnt to a crisp. "Do you still have my shirt?"

"Yeah." She dug it out of her bag and put it on.

Good.

He rounded the point and breathed out a sigh of relief. Finally a bit of luck. The western side had toppled trees, but the receding wave had pulled most of them from the shore and there was a clear sandy section.

The downside was, most of the trees were floating in the bay between them and the shore.

He cut the engine and lifted it from the water.

Mila glanced at him. "What are you doing?"

He grabbed an oar. "We're both going to need to clear the water." He plotted their path to shore and pointed it out to her.

As they rowed, he considered the next steps. It would be difficult to carry the boat through the greenery in order to hide it, but he didn't want to deflate it in case they needed a quick getaway.

So that left hiding it in plain sight and hoping no boats or aircraft coming this way would notice it.

Anything out of the ordinary would catch the searchers' attention.

He brought them right onto the sandy beach next to some trees.

He jumped off and then helped Mila disembark. She whistled and Trixie leapt off the boat and came to heel.

She exhaled, straightened her shoulders and asked, "What now?"

"I want to camouflage the boat and make it appear as if it's part of the debris." He pulled it higher up the shore until he was happy the tide wouldn't drag it out, cleaned out the dog vomit, and spread branches and leaves over the boat. "Then we regroup. I want to try the team. They'll be back on the ship by now." The satellite phone was a last resort, but there was also no other way to contact base without Radar's sig gear.

He helped her over to the shade of the forest. "Rest your ankle."

She winced as she put some pressure on it, so it was probably hurting her more than she wanted to admit.

When the boat was covered, he placed his pack on his back, covered their sign on the sand and then joined her, scanning the forest. "We need to get under cover." He picked her up in his arms.

Trixie growled.

Shit.

"No, Trixie," Mila said.

The dog continued to growl, posture stiff. Dobby had worked with some military dogs in the past and though Trixie wasn't well-trained, he gave the hand command to stand down. Trixie relaxed and so did he.

He carried Mila further into the forest, looking for a place she could rest. It was the same as the rainforest of the region, large trees, palms and vines, and leaf litter on the ground.

She only had her strappy sandals and with her sprained ankle, she wouldn't be able to walk far. "Rest here." He handed her the canteen of water. "I'm going to scout the island, see if there's anything useful." And ensure it was deserted. "I might be an hour."

Her wide eyes showed her concern, but she nodded. "Plan F?"

Beyond exhausted.

"Something like that." He pulled her in for a hug. "You're doing amazing, Mila. Hang in there. We'll be out of here soon."

"Damien?"

He liked hearing her say his name. Most people

called him by his nickname, but it felt right hearing his name from her.

She pressed her lips together. "Are your team likely to come back for us?"

"They'll want to." That he could guarantee.

"But they may not be permitted to," she answered for him. "Where were they headed?"

"We were doing friendly manoeuvres off the coast. They'll have gone back to the ship to stabilise Hawk. One of the doctors on board should be able to help him."

"The government will send a relief team to the area," Mila said. "They've done it before."

He nodded. "They may have dropped personnel in the main village as cover for picking up the team. If that's the case, the boat will be back to support them, but it will take time to arrive."

"And if they didn't?"

"Then the ship will sail past and head for the mainland." The relief efforts would be concentrated on the more populated areas, rather than the three small islands around them.

She glanced around. "So we wait here until it arrives?"

"I'm going to find the highest point so I can get a clear view of the surrounding ocean to see who's around. Then I'll call the ship." He wasn't sure what his reception would be and he didn't want to worry Mila.

She sank down on the ground. "We're not safe yet, are we?"

"Not yet. Not until we get you on the ship."

She closed her eyes.

Guilt sparked in his chest. He'd asked a lot of her over the past twelve hours. "Scootch down on the floor and rest." He dug into his pack and handed her a camouflage sheet. "Lay on this."

"When are you going to rest?"

"Don't worry about me. I can go days with no sleep." He smiled.

She groaned. "I don't know how you do it." She lay down and looked at him. "Thank you for saving me, Damien."

His heart pinched. "Any time."

Trixie lay down next to her, and she put her arm around the dog, drawing comfort. Dobby gave the dog the sign to guard, but it didn't respond.

Still he was fairly sure the dog would protect Mila if its earlier growl was any indication.

He waited until she closed her eyes before he exhaled. He was far too attached.

He left her with the water and a protein bar, and gave some jerky to Trixie, but took his pack and rifle with him and travelled inland. The cliffs which faced the main island would give him the height he needed, and the ground sloped in that direction.

About ten minutes later the ground shifted up at a steep angle so he walked along the base until he found somewhere he could keep climbing.

Checking his compass, he adjusted his course and ten minutes later reached the edge of the tree line.

Black rocks stretched a few metres further from the tree line with some bushes scrabbling for purchase, but from here he could see across the ocean to the main island.

A large boat was on the horizon, coming from Sumatra. More help was on the way.

Dobby retrieved his scope and the satellite phone and scanned the western horizon where they'd been playing war games.

Clear.

He sighed and called the number, giving the codes that were required.

"Patrol six six alpha, what is your status?"

"Have Angel and zod and ready for extraction."

"Hold."

Dobby kept scanning the area while he waited and finally Radar's voice came over sounding delighted. "Patrol six six alpha confirm Angel is Hawk's Angel?"

Dobby grinned. "Confirmed."

"Sun God will rendezvous at drop zone at twenty-two hundred."

Dobby exhaled in relief. "Copy. Bring a Lassie loop."

"Can't wait to see why." Radar chuckled, but in the background Dobby heard demands for more information.

Dobby signed off before he could be told not to bring Trixie with him.

His superior officer was going to be so pissed with him. Abandoning a mission, going rogue, not making the rendezvous.

He'd be lucky if he didn't get demoted.

The idea didn't worry him as much as it would have a few years ago. Maybe it really was time to get out.

If they demoted him, he could resign and start a personal security company. One where he chose his assignments.

He smiled. And he could set up the company wherever he wanted.

The thought of living near Mila, wherever that was, was appealing.

He shook his head. They were thoughts for the future, when they were both safe.

Right now he needed to ensure they stayed safe until extraction.

The beach he'd left Mila near faced west, but he'd prefer to have a wider range of vision in case they were discovered. He needed to find somewhere to camp which kept them close to the zod as well.

A breeze blew from the west, cooling the sweat on his skin and he lifted his face to it. He couldn't relax fully, but he could rest his aching muscles. He sipped water from his pack and ate a protein bar.

Dobby hoped Hawk was all right. He would have months of recovery and Dobby wasn't sure how he'd handle it. He didn't have family to help him.

Maybe that was another reason to get out. To help his mate. Perhaps they could build a new security firm together.

Something to think about when he was home, back in his own bed.

He gave the horizon another scan and moved back into the trees, heading the opposite way from which he'd come to check the rest of the island.

This mission had been the icing on the shit show of the past couple of missions. Someone was pulling strings high up to send them places they shouldn't be going.

No, that wasn't quite right. Special ops was all about going places no one should go, but the reasons for doing it—like saving Vance when he'd faked his own kidnapping—were not ones he could get behind.

He'd wanted to help people, and it felt like the missions were more about someone's private agenda.

He sighed. It wasn't his job to know why he was sent in, and there were reasons above his pay grade, but the work had lost its appeal. That's why he hadn't been able to leave Mila behind. She'd been worthy of saving, not Vance.

They wouldn't have found Hawk in time if it wasn't for her. She was selfless, caring and so strong.

He would protect her at any cost.

The strength of his emotion surprised him, but he'd examine it later.

Before he returned to Mila, he scouted for a place to camp. It was just after midday, and he'd noticed a bank of clouds on the horizon telling him it would rain before the day ended.

He found a place on the point where he could see the zod and to the south-west and was surrounded by enough trees that they shouldn't be spotted. He cleared a space and set up a shelter between two trees so when he fetched Mila she could go right back to sleep.

When he returned to her, she wasn't sleeping. She leaned against a tree, knees pulled into her chest, arms around Trixie and looked relieved to see him.

"Damien."

He smiled, though he didn't like the fear in her voice. "Everything OK?"

She nodded and then shook her head. "Bad dream."

"Well I can cheer you up. I've set up camp and we've got an extraction time."

Relief filled her expression. "When?"

"Twenty-two hundred." He offered her his hand to help her up. "I'll carry you."

She didn't refuse, just wrapped her arms and legs around him and clung to him like a warm hug. Her hands trembled and he kissed one, his heart aching for what she'd been through. "We're going to be fine."

She was his mission now.

***

Tears were far too close to the surface and Mila blinked to stop them from spilling over as she clung to Damien's back. Exhaustion was a thick fog surrounding her. The only thing that calmed her was being close to Damien. She tightened her hold around him, not ever wanting to let him go.

He was her safe space.

The dream she'd had—the nightmare—had been

175

watching Damien being washed away by the tsunami and being unable to stop it.

She hadn't even cared she'd been caught in the water.

She'd only wanted to save him.

The water had sucked her under and as she was about to run out of air, Trixie had nudged her awake.

The dog's wet fur had been a comfort as she clung to her. But though the dog had snuggled in, the panic hadn't disappeared until she'd stared into Dobby's beautiful eyes.

So what did that tell her? That she loved him?

No. This type of situation was about heightened emotions. She shouldn't read anything into her dreams. She barely knew Damien.

But afterwards… perhaps he wouldn't mind if she looked him up.

Special ops were based on the west coast and she lived in the east so it wouldn't be easy.

"Here we are. Home sweet home." He let her down and she looked past him at the camp he'd built them.

He'd set up a waterproof sheet as a tent low to the ground between two trees and placed large palm leaves over it to help it blend in. He'd lined the space with fresh leaves and his pack was to one side.

A safe space for now.

She swallowed the lump in her throat and smiled. "Cosy."

"It might rain later so I wanted to make sure we had shelter. The sides can come down to give us more protection."

She groaned. "It will definitely rain later." She should have thought of it.

He chuckled and held back the flap for her to crawl inside. She bit her lip, butterflies swirling around her chest.

"What's the plan?" She shifted to a comfortable position as Trixie lay down outside the shelter but close to her.

"We'll take the zod to the original drop zone and they'll pick us up."

She closed her eyes. They were finally getting out of there. "The next time I see Vance, I'm punching him in the face."

That chuckle again as he joined her under the tent, leaning back against the tree trunk and stretching his legs out next to hers. "I didn't take you to be the violent sort, sweetheart."

Every time he called her that, her heart did a little pitter-patter. She embraced it and answered. "If it wasn't for him, neither of us would be in this situation. If he hadn't faked his kidnapping, you wouldn't be here and Ethan wouldn't be injured, and if he hadn't told Agus who my parents were, I could have stayed on the island and helped with the clean-up."

"Yeah, but then we would have never met, and that would have been a damn shame."

She placed a hand to her chest. His words were like a caress to her soul. "You're such a sweet talker."

"Only with you." His eyes were full of emotion.

She didn't care if what she was feeling was due to heightened emotions. Right now all she wanted was him.

Before she'd even processed the thought she was across the other side of the tent, straddling him and with her lips pressed against his. It took him only a second to respond and his hands roved over her back as he pulled her closer.

Heat, passion, emotion.

She couldn't get enough of him as she tugged his shirt free of his pants and his hands slipped up to cup her breast.

The bandage was too thick. She couldn't feel the slow flick of his thumb over her nipple as much as she wanted to.

She fought to strip off her shirt and then her dress. With a deft hand she fished the multi-tool from her cleavage and tackled the bandage.

Damien chuckled. "Where'd you get that?"

"My mother. Came in handy cutting the sheets." Finally the bandage fell away.

His eyes darkened. "Sweetheart, you're breath-taking, but maybe we shouldn't." Gently he brushed the purpling bruises on her skin. "You must hurt all over."

She shook her head. "I need this."

He searched her eyes and then leaned forward, taking her breast in his mouth and she gasped, throwing her head back.

This. This was what she needed.

His hand slid beneath her underwear and he brushed her clit.

Too much.

Was there such a thing?

She tried to tackle the buttons of his shirt but her fingers weren't coordinated enough, so instead she just shoved it up and let her hands roam over his hard abs.

A washboard forged in steel. She wanted to run her tongue all over it, but he captured her mouth with his again and all she could do was hold on while he pleasured her. She shifted so she could rub against his erection and he used the opportunity to slide his finger inside of her.

"Oh!"

"Come for me, sweetheart," he murmured in her ear before he nipped it and kissed down her neck.

"I, oh." No words would form. She wanted him inside her, but his fingers had found the right spot, teasing and thrusting. The wave of passion built and her head flung back as it overtook her.

"You are incredible," Damien whispered as he kissed her one more time.

She felt incredible, but she wanted more. She wanted him naked, wanted him deep inside her.

She nipped at his lips. "I'm not finished yet." Her hands found his belt, but he stopped her.

"You don't have to do this."

Surprise had her leaning back. "But I want to. Don't you want me to?"

His strangled laugh made her concern fade. "More than you know, but it's been a stressful time for you."

She scowled at him. "Don't tell me I don't know my own body or what I want." Though the chivalry was sweet on him.

"I wouldn't dare."

"And you want me as much as I want you?" she confirmed.

He nodded. "More."

She grinned. "We'll see about that. Now where in that hulking pack of yours are the condoms?"

He raised his eyebrows in a question.

"I know they're standard issue. Gimme." She gestured to the pack, and he shifted, lifting her with him as he did, and pulled the pack towards them. In moments he had a condom in his hand and then he flipped them so she was on her back and he was on top of her.

"Are you sure?"

"Positive," she promised.

***

Mila's declaration sent a shot of lust through Dobby. The way she'd responded to him had made him so hard and he desperately wanted to be inside her.

And she wanted him too.

He'd worried this was a response from the stressful situation and didn't want to take advantage of her, but the determination in her eyes told him she wanted this as much as he did.

He lay over her, mindful it wasn't a soft mattress beneath them and kept most of his weight off her. "This OK?"

She grinned. "Only if you stop talking and get to work."

He laughed, amazed he could, but Mila made everything so much better. She had an optimism and a way of seeing the world that spoke to him.

Out of habit, he checked their surroundings though he knew they were alone. Then he turned his attention to the perfection lying below him.

Her lips were already plump from their kisses and he brushed another kiss over them. Her taste was addictive, sweet and drugging and he deepened the kiss while his hands roamed over her body.

Mila's moan sent thrills through his body, making him harder than he already was. He wouldn't last long when he got inside her. He wanted her too much.

Dobby trailed kisses down her body, savouring her delectable small breasts as she groaned. He kissed down her belly, all the way to the juncture of her thighs and licked her clit. Her breathy pants drove him crazy.

"Damien, more."

He was helpless to resist her pleas. He finished stripping down his pants and slid on the condom. He hovered over her and waited until her eyes fluttered open. Then he thrust deep inside her.

Warm, wet softness.

Perfection.

Bliss.

They groaned together and Mila shifted her hips to take him deeper. He paused a moment to stamp this feeling and image on his memory, and then moved slowly, extracting gasps and pants from this beautiful woman who had captured his heart in such a short time.

The realisation of how much she meant to him made him slow, savour, wanting this to last for hours in case this was the only time they did this.

Mila made a sound of complaint. "Faster."

"Not this time, sweetheart. I want to enjoy every inch of you."

She pouted, then gasped and arched her back as he thrust deeper inside her. She was the image of a Goddess, everything perfect from her green eyes, to her luscious lips, down past the most perfect breasts and right down to her toes.

Her scratches and bruises only added to her power, showing him how strong she was.

He continued his slow thrusts as her moans became faster and louder. When he was certain her orgasm was close, he increased his speed.

"Yes!" she cried, wrapping her legs around his waist and he thrust harder and faster as his own orgasm hit him.

Heart pumping, he continued to move until he was certain Mila was thoroughly satisfied.

He leaned forward and kissed her, rolling them sideways so he could hold her close.

"That was amazing," Mila breathed.

He smiled, unable to find the right words to describe what it had meant to him.

She lifted her head to look at him. "Damien? You still alive?"

He laughed, a little bemused. He'd never laughed after sex before. "Just basking." He hugged her and then reluctantly let her go to clean up.

When they were clothed, he leaned against the tree

trunk and pulled Mila back into his arms.

He stroked her arms, unable to stop touching her.

She snuggled in and it warmed his heart. "Where do you live, Damien?"

The question caught him by surprise. "Perth."

"Do you get over to Sydney very often?"

"A couple of times a year." He shifted so he could see her face. "Is that where you're from?"

She nodded. "I was thinking I'd like to do this with you again... and again."

Though his heart soared, he kept his words light. "What, get caught in a tsunami, chased by someone who wants to kidnap you and get stuck on a deserted island?"

She groaned. "No, none of that."

"Have crazy good sex on a deserted island?" he asked.

"The crazy good sex, yes, but maybe in a five-star hotel where there's hot water, showers and a soft bed."

"I'm glad Agus found you some decent clothes."

"I like wearing your shirt."

Oh, he was really gone. "I like seeing you in my shirt."

"What's it like in special ops?" Mila asked. "Do you have to drop everything at a moment's notice?"

"Sometimes," he said. "Other times it's day-to-day training."

"Is it difficult to have a normal life?"

"We can get deployed for long periods at times which is hard for partners. We can't tell them where we're going and often can't contact them at all."

Were these questions just to make conversation, or did she really want to know about his life? Should he read something into that? "What will you do now?"

She shrugged. "I hadn't thought past getting off the island. I would have stayed to help with the recovery, but Agus has taken that option away from me."

He squeezed her. "Many people survived because of you. That's the most important thing."

"I know but it feels as if I'm abandoning them." She sighed. "I don't have any job to get back to in Sydney."

Dobby hesitated, not sure whether he should say anything. No, he took calculated risks every day. "There might be jobs on the west coast." He held his breath.

She glanced up at him, her eyes searching his. "Would you like that?"

"Yeah."

They looked at each other for a long moment, each of them searching for something in the other's eyes. Finally Mila nodded. "I'll have to see what's available."

Warmth spread through him. He kept the conversation light. "Do you have any siblings?"

"Two older brothers, one in the army, the other works with Dad."

He smiled. "You took your own path." But it reminded him. "Where did you learn how to get out of restraints?"

"My brother, Jared. He taught me when he learnt how to in the army."

"Remind me to thank him."

She nodded. "What's your family like?"

"A younger sister, currently engaged to a real idiot. I'm hoping she'll see his true colours before the wedding." But he doubted it. "And an older sister who is married and has twin girls." He smiled. "They're adorable but I don't get to see them as much as I'd like." He shrugged. "Dad drives trucks and Mum's a bookkeeper."

He waited for her reaction. He'd dated a couple of women who'd turned up their noses at his parents.

"I've always wondered what it's like to drive trucks all day. Does he get bored?"

Dobby's muscles relaxed, and he shook his head. "He's the most well-read person I know. Listens to audiobooks all day."

"Bliss," Mila responded. "I bet he's an interesting person to talk to."

And just like that, Dobby fell in love with her.

Chapter 15

Mila snuggled deeper into Damien's warm, strong arms. For the first time since she'd seen Vance on the island, she felt happy. She could pretend they were on a date as they got to know each other.

Trixie lay within arm's reach and dozed.

Damien had saved the dog for her, though she wasn't sure what they would do with her now. A problem they could discuss before they left for the rendezvous, but right now she wanted to bask in the good feelings.

Damien's suggestion to move to Perth was tempting. She wanted to learn everything about him, though she wasn't certain she would be suited to life as a military wife. It was hard when her mother missed special occasions and now with her brother in the army, they rarely had a Christmas together.

The humidity increased, and she shifted away from him and reached for the canteen. In the distance the bank of rain clouds was getting closer. "Rain will hit soon."

"Yeah. It will make it more difficult for extraction. Tropical storms are full of lightning."

She shuddered. "I don't want to be responsible for a helicopter being struck down."

"The rain should ease by twenty-two hundred."

He got out an MRE. "You hungry?"

She nodded. The rice porridge seemed an age ago.

"After we've eaten, you can sleep," Damien said.

"Only if you do."

He smiled. "You first."

She didn't know how he did it. She'd been in a lovely hazy cocoon since they'd had sex and wouldn't have been able to react fast if Agus had found them and stormed the camp.

Damien took a few mouthfuls of the MRE and then handed it to her. He hadn't got another one out.

"Are we sharing?"

He nodded.

Right. In case something unexpected happened and they were here for longer. Always planning for contingencies.

Trixie's ears perked up, and she shifted closer. Dobby passed her some jerky and then poured water into a cup so she could drink.

Mila smiled. "Thank you for rescuing her."

He snorted. "I didn't have much choice with the two of you begging me."

He was such a softie.

"Can't we extract her too?"

"I asked Radar to bring a sling." Damien shrugged. "But it depends on how well she's been trained. She might freak out when the helicopter comes and lash out."

Mila took a bite of the meal. She hadn't thought past saving Trixie from drowning, but he was right. A helicopter might be terrifying for the dog.

She stroked Trixie's fur.

"You need to be prepared that we might have to

leave her behind."

Where she'd starve to death.

Dread pitted in her stomach and she handed Damien the remainder of the MRE packet. Perhaps she'd done the wrong thing. Trixie would have turned around and swum back to shore eventually.

"I'm sorry, Mila."

She nodded. "I understand. You didn't expect to be extracting me, let alone a dog." She smiled to show she didn't blame him and the smile turned into a yawn.

He chuckled. "Bedtime."

"Yes, sir." She was too tired to argue with him. Perhaps when she woke, she could work with Trixie and get her used to the idea of a harness. She lay down on the bed of leaves and made herself as comfortable as possible.

And fell asleep.

The heavy drips of rain woke Mila. She blinked, trying to figure out where she was as she spotted the rain pelting down just beyond the forest in the fading light. Not her bedroom, and not anywhere she recognised.

"Sleep well?"

She rolled over at Damien's voice as everything came into focus. Her heart rate slowed seeing him sitting across from her in his black fatigues, a small smile on his face.

She nodded and sat up as the rain trickled through the foliage above and hit the shelter.

"What time is it?" It was darker now but more than the clouds could explain.

"Almost eighteen hundred."

She stared at him. "You let me sleep all afternoon?"

"Yeah. You needed it."

"So do you." She was tired of him refusing to rest. "That's it. You're sleeping and I'm standing guard. If anyone calls, I'll wake you. If someone comes into the bay, I'll wake you. But right now, you are going to sleep."

He hauled her into his arms. "You're gorgeous when you're bossy."

She squirmed, not sure he was taking her seriously until he said, "If you're worried about anything, you wake me."

She nodded.

"I've been working with Trixie. She knows a lot of hand signals." He demonstrated and Trixie obeyed his commands. "You try."

"How do you know them?"

"I've worked with military dogs in the past."

She followed his lead and Trixie sat, stood and turned around at her command. Mila frowned. "If she's so well trained, why didn't she attack us?"

"They might have given her a follow command rather than an attack command."

"She doesn't have a tracker on her, does she?"

Dobby scowled. "Not that I can find. If she did, Agus would have come to get us by now." He handed her his helmet with a pair of goggles on them. "Stay vigilant though. These are night vision goggles if you need them."

"Thanks." She shifted so he could stretch out.

"Wake me in an hour."

"Three," she countered. She wanted him to sleep as long as possible.

"Two or we'll miss the rendezvous."

She nodded. Not something she wanted to do.

He closed his eyes and in only moments he was fast asleep.

Mila glanced out at the pouring rain. She was sweaty and a little dirty from their escape, and the water looked inviting. No one was around to see her. She stripped off her dress and underpants and put them on top of Damien's pack. Then she carefully made her way to the edge of the forest and into the downpour.

The warm drops drenched her immediately, and she grinned, turning her face to the sky to embrace it for a moment before she started rubbing the sweat from her body, starting with her face and moving down her arms, her torso and to her legs.

This time she took her time, luxuriating in a shower she didn't have to rush, one where she didn't have to worry about someone bursting in on her.

When she was satisfied, she returned to the shelter where she met Damien's gaze. Heat filled her cheeks. "You're supposed to be sleeping."

"And miss that sexy show? No way."

She screwed her nose up at him and used the damp hand towel still in her bag to dry herself before dressing again and putting Damien's shirt over the top to protect her from insect bites.

She leaned down and kissed him. "Sleep."

"Yes, ma'am."

His breathing slowed. She hung the hand towel and her other clothes from one of the string lines Damien had set up, though she didn't expect them to dry in this humidity. Then she settled in to wait.

Two hours later, the rain had stopped as had the chorus of frogs, and the only sound was the occasional drip of water through the canopy. The satellite phone rang.

Before Mila could reach forward to wake Damien, he lunged up and grabbed the phone, his eyes only slightly sleepy. "Copy."

Wow. What a reaction. Here was the well-trained soldier.

He nodded and then repeated some coordinates. "Copy."

Damien hung up and grinned at her. "We're going home."

His smile was infectious, and she grinned as she untied the other side of the shelter.

In only a minute the camp was packed. Damien scanned the area to make sure they hadn't left anything behind and then swept her up in his arms. "I'll carry you."

She didn't waste her breath arguing, just wound her arms around his neck and snuggled in.

"Heel, Trixie." The dog fell into step as Damien nuzzled Mila's hair.

This was the end of their private interlude. Part of her longed to stay here and not return to the real world.

Would she and Damien have a chance out there?

At the shore it took little time to uncover the boat and launch it, Trixie jumping in with ease.

"I need you as spotter at the front," he said.

She shifted into position with her oar and directed him through the still water, past the point and out into the open ocean. As they cleared the islet, she looked back towards the main island.

Everything was dark. It would be a while before power was restored. As she watched, a light blinked on. She frowned. "What's that?"

It looked like they were the lights of a boat, but it was pretty late for anyone to be leaving.

Damien glanced over. "Boat." He increased his speed and she kept her eyes on the water for obstacles.

"Do we need to be worried?"

"Shouldn't concern us."

Something in his voice was off. She glanced back but couldn't see his expression well in the darkness. She checked their route and then glanced back at the main island.

More lights. The boat had lights on three decks.

Agus's luxury cruiser.

She shook her head. That couldn't be a coincidence. She had heard stories of him going away at night and coming back a few days later with the spoils of his outing.

But why tonight?

Unless he wanted to get away from the island and the pressure to help with clean up. Or he had a radar on board and was waiting for them to make a move.

That sounded like him.

They cleared the thickest part of the floating debris and Damien accelerated again.

Mila glanced behind to find the cruiser heading straight out to sea towards them. "Damien?"

He gestured her closer so she could hear him. "I see them. They might just be taking the easiest route out of the bay before they change direction."

She hoped that was the case. "Or they may have radar and are checking out who we are?"

He nodded.

"How far to extraction?"

"Another couple of kilometres. The ship's been diverted and we have different coordinates to reach. If Agus is still following us, we'll have to do it fast."

She hugged her torso and glanced at Trixie. "What does that mean?"

"Depends on the helo they send. They send the Chinook and we'll drive straight in and take off. If they send something smaller, we might just get winched up."

"What about the boat?"

"Collateral damage." He shrugged. "They'll send down either a sling or a ladder. The ladder you climb as fast as you can. The sling goes over your torso and under your arms. They'll haul you up."

Her gut clenched. Not something she wanted to do while being chased but this was all in a day's work for

Damien. "And Trixie?"

"I'll deal with her."

He got on the radio. "Radar, you copy?"

"Copy."

"We've got a possible bogie following us. We'll need to do it fast."

"Copy."

Agus's boat was still heading towards them.

A loud thud had Mila grabbing the side and glancing forward. Another debris field. Damien slowed and she scrambled to the bow to direct him through it. This one was as thick as the one closer to the island and they had to slow to a crawl. Frantically she used the oar to shift larger trees and planks out of the way.

She glanced back.

Agus's boat had halved the distance between them.

Where was the helicopter?

The sky in front of them was dark. Would it be running lights? Possibly not.

Damien increased the speed again as the debris thinned. Mila checked where Agus was. The distance had halved again. Perhaps he didn't think the debris would damage his boat.

A whump, whump noise was faint to her ears. She scanned the sky again and Damien flashed a light on then off, on then off again.

Finally she spotted the dark shape in the sky. It was coming in low and Damien accelerated again so they were out of the debris field.

He put on his night vision goggles. "Get ready," he shouted.

She crouched in the bow of the boat as the helicopter came directly overhead. The noise was deafening and water flung up stinging her eyes. Agus was now only a couple of hundred metres away.

Trixie cowered.

Mila stroked her while searching for the ladder, but the wind from the rotor blades spat up water around her and made it hard to see anything.

Damien grabbed her, threaded a loop over her head and under her arms and yelled, "Hold on!" He said something into the radio and she was jerked off the boat.

No! She couldn't leave him behind.

Damien bent to the dog and then she couldn't see him any more as strong arms hoisted her into the helicopter.

Joker grinned at her. "Nice to see you again."

"Damien!"

"He'll be right with us." Joker pressed her into a seat and strapped her in.

She glanced to the door as the line that had brought her up started rising again.

Damien appeared holding a very nervous Trixie in his arms. A soldier she didn't recognise grabbed Trixie's collar and pulled her aboard. Mila waved her hands to get the dog's attention, and the soldier clipped on a lead and handed it to her. She stroked the dog's fur as she waited for Damien to climb in.

Her breath exploded from her as Radar slammed the door shut and the helicopter raced away.

Damien slapped hands with his teammates and then sat next to her, pulling her into his arms. "You're safe now."

She closed her eyes and sobbed.

***

Mila curled into Dobby's arms on the ride back to the ship. It was too loud to talk, but he noticed the questioning looks from his team. He had to admit if he'd been in their position, he would have had the same expression on his face, but right now he didn't care what they thought.

Connor, aka Lassie, one of the dog handlers, sat with Trixie, tempting her with a treat until she sat and leaned into him.

The helicopter came in to land and Dobby helped Mila off. He carried her, mindful of her ankle, as he jogged with his men towards the doors inside.

As he placed her on the ground, a uniformed man raced out from a doorway. Mila screeched and threw her arms around him. He hugged her, bending down to talk in her ear.

The thick instant jealousy almost choked Damien until they pulled apart and he noticed the man's name on his shirt.

Watkins. Mila's brother.

Hell, he hadn't realised he was on board.

Watkins tried to drag her inside, but she stopped him and turned back to the team. "How's Ethan?"

"He's stable. He'll fly home tomorrow," Axle said.

"Can I visit him?"

"He'd like that," Radar told her.

The rotors shut down, and the noise reduced. "Command wants to know what happened." Watkins glanced at Damien.

Joker leaned closer. "They're not happy."

Of course they weren't. They had to spend extra resources to pick him up.

"Thanks for getting my sister out of there." Watkins offered Dobby his hand and Dobby shook it. "These guys told me what they could, and Vance gave his side of the story." The man rolled his eyes.

"No problem. She should get her scratches examined by a doctor to make sure they don't get infected and she has a sprained ankle and stitches in her arm." He could still picture her washing in the rain. It was an image he would never forget. "She could also do with a hot shower and clean clothes."

"I'll make sure she gets it."

"Damien needs the same," Mila piped up. "He's barely slept."

Her brother raised his eyebrows at them both, but said to his sister, "He needs to report in first. Come with me."

Mila looked at Dobby and he nodded though he wasn't ready to let her go. "I'll catch up with you later." Their private time was over.

She nodded and followed her brother into the ship.

"Where did you get the dog?" Connor asked, crouching down to stroke the uncertain animal. He glanced up, his blond fringe falling into his eyes and he pushed it back with impatience.

"It was the kidnapper's. It followed us into the ocean while we were escaping and Mila made me rescue it."

Connor grinned. "Like you would have let it drown."

If it had threatened Mila, he would have. "It's got training."

Connor nodded. "I'll check her. She'll need quarantining from the rest of the dogs, but I'll work something out."

Dobby smiled. He knew he'd have an ally with Connor.

"What the hell happened?" Joker asked as Dobby's team moved into the ship to the communal room they'd been using.

Before he could respond a corporal came to the door. "Sergeant Dobson, the Major wants to see you immediately."

Christ. That was the last thing he wanted right now. "I'll fill you in when I get back," he told his team and followed the corporal into the bowels of the ship.

Major Hammond was a humourless, by-the-book man who expected absolute perfection from his men.

This wouldn't be fun.

He adjusted his uniform, checking the buttons on his shirt were done up correctly and tucking it in. He was still filthy, but it was the best he could do without a shower and fresh clothes.

The room he entered contained not only Major Hammond but also the Colonel and the Major-General, unfortunately not Mila's mother.

Shit.

Dobby saluted.

"At ease," the major said.

"Did you extract Mila Watkins?" the Major-General asked.

"Yes, sir. Her brother is taking her to the infirmary and then to get cleaned up."

"Would you like to explain why you thought it important to abandon your mission to rescue her?" the colonel asked, his tone deceptively mild.

"She helped us rescue Ethan Ward and lured Vance Bradley's kidnappers away from their home so we could be evacuated. Vance exposed her parentage to the kidnappers, which made her a valuable commodity." He paused to let that sink in. "I deemed she was at risk of being taken hostage and as she is an Australian citizen, I saw it fit to offer my assistance to extract her from the island."

"Explain in detail," the Major-General barked.

Dobby gritted his teeth. This was going to take some time.

Chapter 16

Mila glanced back at Damien as Jared took her into the ship, but he was already talking to his teammates. It was harder to leave him than she'd anticipated. Foolish, she hadn't prepared herself for it, but she hadn't considered what would happen after they arrived on the ship.

At least her brother was here. She squeezed his hand as she limped down the corridor. She hadn't heard where he'd been going on his latest deployment so seeing him had been an incredible shock.

"Are you OK, Milly?" he asked.

"I am now. Damien didn't say anything about you being here."

"He didn't know. I didn't hear about the tsunami until the team got back and said you were in danger. Command dragged me in when they couldn't get a hold of Mum." He stepped into a bathroom and handed her clean army fatigues. "Take a shower and then I'll get you to the infirmary."

"Does Mum know I'm safe?"

He nodded. "Mum eventually got in touch with the Major-General and he's kept her informed as a matter of courtesy."

He closed the door as he left and she looked around the small room. Safe. Finally.

She closed her eyes as the tears welled and her chest squeezed.

Damien had promised he'd get her out, and he had.

She took a long, shuddery breath and stripped off her clothes, stepping under the steaming shower.

The heat melted away the rest of her resistance and she slid to the floor and cried.

A knock on the door had her heart racing. "You alive in there, Milly?"

She smiled at her brother's voice and swallowed hard, brushing away the tears. "Yeah. Won't be long." She washed her face and the rest of the dirt from her and switched off the shower.

When she wiped the steam from the mirror, her red eyes exposed she'd been crying. No matter. Her brother would understand.

She dressed and opened the door. Jared took one look at her and his expression grew pained. He dragged her into his arms. "Milly, I can't imagine what you've been through."

Tears threatened again, and she swallowed them down, hugging him back. "I'm OK. I'll be OK." It might take her a while to realise it was the truth, but it was the truth, nonetheless.

He seemed reluctant to let her go. "Hungry?"

"As long as it's not an MRE," she said.

He laughed. "You got the real experience, didn't you?"

She nodded.

"I'll organise something for you, but you need to be examined by the doctor first." Jared helped her to a large infirmary and waited while all her cuts were sanitised, and her ankle was examined.

"How did you get the cuts?" the doctor asked.

"Most were from getting caught in the tsunami," Mila said.

"What?" Jared's shout made her jump.

She frowned. "Didn't they tell you?"

He shook his head. "All they told me was you were on the island with one of the team."

The doctor frowned. "Did you swallow any water?"

"Yeah, but I vomited it up."

"How long ago?"

"It must be about twenty-four hours by now."

"I still need to scan your lungs and stomach." The doctor gave an order to the nurse in the room.

In no time Mila was being scanned and the doctor was checking the results. He smiled. "There's no cause for concern. It doesn't appear as if any of the water damaged your lungs."

That was a relief.

The doctor gave her some crutches and dismissed her.

"I want to hear about everything," Jared said as he took her to the mess. At this time of night there weren't many people inside and he made her a sandwich. "What happened?"

Mila sighed. No doubt she'd have to tell her story dozens of times over the next few days. "I didn't have time to thank the team who rescued me. Do you think they're awake?"

Jared smiled at her. "I can almost guarantee they'll be waiting until Dobby has finished explaining things to his CO."

She bit her lip. "How much trouble will he be in?"

"Hard to say. Mum might pull a few strings, though she doesn't like doing it."

"Should I call her?"

"We'll need permission for the call and she's

deployed at the moment. I'll put in a request. Now will you tell me what happened?"

She smiled. "Can I tell you at the same time as I tell the team? They'll want to know what occurred after they left."

Jared sighed and gestured to her. She followed him down the sparse corridors to a rec room where Radar, Joker and Axle waited. It was a sparse area with grey walls and seating bolted to the floor.

"This is my brother, Jared," she said.

Joker grinned. "We've met. He was pretty insistent about keeping informed about your whereabouts."

Mila watched a faint blush tint her brother's cheeks. "Were you?"

He grimaced. "I needed to make sure my baby sister was all right."

She hugged him. "I am thanks to these men and Damien." She turned to the men. "Thank you." She hugged each of them in turn, though Radar squirmed a bit.

"You helped to get us out of there with Hawk and Vance," Joker said. "We should be thanking you."

She'd forgotten about her ex. "Where is Vance?"

"Sleeping," Radar said. "He's heading out on the same flight as Hawk."

"You'll probably be on the same flight," Jared said.

"That might not be safe for Vance," she murmured and Joker laughed.

"So what the hell happened?" Jared demanded. "Last I heard you were teaching English and had split up with Vance. But he swore he went to get you back when I saw him earlier."

Her cheeks heated. "Vance never had a hope in hell," she retorted. "He was using me to get a job in Dad's company. What he did was sell me out to the local smuggler who hates Mum, and who stole my phone and computer the day before the tsunami hit so I couldn't contact anyone."

Jared's expression darkened. "Did he now?" The danger in his words reminded her that her brother had a whole other life in the army she didn't know about.

"Then the earthquake hit and I was helping people who were trapped when I ran into the team and told them where I thought Vance was. When the tsunami hit, they were fleeing the town in a four-wheel drive and Ethan fell out. We both got caught in the water, but I wasn't injured."

He turned to her. "Why the hell were you still in town when the tsunami hit?"

Joker nodded his agreement. "She was too busy helping people and then an old woman stole her moped as she was about to escape."

A vein throbbed in her brother's forehead and Mila hurried to explain everything that had occurred over the past twenty-four hours, leaving out the bit about having amazing sex with Damien.

She didn't want to traumatise her brother.

By the end of it, Jared was sitting, shaking his head. He glanced at her. "You're a bad ass, Milly."

"We were pretty impressed by her," Joker agreed. "Which is why we had no problems with Dobby going off mission to rescue her."

"I need to thank him again when I see him," Jared said.

Mila yawned, her eyes heavy. It didn't seem to matter she'd slept the afternoon away, she was still tired.

"Come on, I'll show you to your quarters," Jared said, taking her arm.

She shook her head. "I'm not going until I make sure Damien's all right."

"They won't keel-haul him," Jared joked. "I'm pretty

sure they've done away with that punishment."

"I don't care. I'll wait with the team." She glanced at them. "If you don't mind."

Radar nodded his approval and Joker and Axle both smiled at her, Joker patting the seat next to him.

She settled in to wait.

It was two hours later before Damien walked into the room accompanied by a corporal. He looked exhausted, but his eyes widened when he saw her. "Why aren't you in bed?"

"I'm waiting for you." She got up so he could have her chair. "What did they say?"

"They're threatening a dishonourable discharge. They say the international implications could have been catastrophic."

Her breath left her. "Are they crazy? They risked international implications rescuing that worthless piece of shit, Vance."

A smile played on his lips. "It's called politics, sweetheart."

This was ridiculous. Dobby deserved a medal not a discharge. "I'll give them politics," Mila said. "Where are they? I want to have a word to them."

Though all the men smiled, none of them, not even her brother, made a move to show her.

She was tired of running from confrontation, of being indecisive and avoiding conflict. That's what got her here in the first place. "Do not test me," Mila snarled. "I've had a terrible twenty-four hours and if someone doesn't show me to these imbeciles right now, I will shout down this boat."

"Milly, you can't order command around. You'll make it worse." Jared smiled.

"Don't patronise me," she snapped. "I know how to talk to these men."

The corporal cleared his throat. "Ah, are you Mila Watkins?"

She spun to him. "Yes, I am."

He fought back a nervous smile. "They want to speak with you too."

She grinned at the apprehensive looks on the team's faces. "Good. Lead the way."

She was ready to fight for the man she loved.

The realisation made her pause, but the rightness swept over her.

It was her turn to protect him.

By the time they reached the room where three very important people were seated around a table, she had controlled her initial outrage. She recognised the insignia on the uniforms; major, colonel and major-general.

Her brother was right, these men wouldn't respond to theatrics or demands so she had to be calm and calculated.

The Major-General nodded at her. "Your mother was pleased to hear you're safe."

Mila smiled. She'd met the man at the fundraiser where she'd met Vance. "Thank you for telling her."

"As you can expect," the man continued, "we need to know what happened, and how Sergeant Dobson was left behind."

"Of course. It was quite a fluid and unpredictable experience." She smiled at the men. "May I sit? It's been an exhausting twenty-four hours."

The colonel gestured to a nearby chair, and she rested her crutches against the table and sat, placing her hands together on the table. "What would you like to know?"

"Tell us what happened in your own words," the colonel invited.

She nodded and took a deep breath as if bracing herself. "Damien and Ethan made contact not long after the earthquake hit," she said. "I'm sorry, I don't know the time. Agus, the man who kidnapped Vance, stole my phone."

"Why?" the major asked.

"He said it was so I could give Vance's proposal the proper consideration." She poured herself a glass of water. "But I suspect it was because Vance told him about my parents and he has a sworn vendetta against my mother. He didn't want me to communicate with anyone off the island until he could figure out what he wanted to do with me."

"When was this?" the Major-General asked.

"The day before the earthquake. I was lying in bed trying to figure out how I could escape the island when the earthquake hit." Before they could ask the obvious question she added, "Agus controls all the boats coming to and leaving the island and I was refused passage on the evening's barge even though it was empty." She paused a moment, so they understood the vulnerable position Vance had put her in. "I suspect if the earthquake hadn't hit, my mother would have received a similar video to the one the Defence Minister received."

Let them stew on that.

"I told your men that Vance had befriended Agus and as far as I knew, he was staying with him at the house on the cliff. I explained the security and the room layout. They left, but Damien told me to head for the mountains so I was out of harm's way."

"Did you?" the colonel asked.

She shook her head. "Every time I was about to leave, I heard someone else cry for help. I couldn't leave them there to drown."

A modicum of respect showed on all three men's

faces.

"Then the tsunami hit. The lady I was helping stole my moped and got out ahead of the wave, but I got caught in it. I saw Ethan fall out of the four-wheel drive just before I went under." She shuddered and hugged herself.

"How did he fall?"

"They were trying to pull him inside. He was on the back, but I guess he must have slipped." She swallowed hard at the memory. "We were fortunate we were at the end of the water's push inland. It turned, sucking everything back to the ocean, and I grabbed onto a tree trunk and hung on until it receded."

"You weren't injured?"

"Battered, bruised and swallowed a heap of dirty water, but alive. I started looking for Ethan immediately and found him by the time the team returned. We had just enough time to find a stretcher for him and get him into the car before the next wave hit."

"It sounds like we owe you a debt of gratitude," the colonel said. "You saved that man's life."

She shook her head. "The team did. Damien had Ethan on the stretcher in what seemed like seconds. He was incredible." A hero.

"What happened next?"

Mila continued to tell them the story, talking Damien up, and emphasising what she had done to get them off the island. When she spoke about Agus's men trying to stop her from leaving, they glanced at each other.

"Honestly if Damien hadn't come after me, I'm not sure what Agus would have done to me. He might have just held me hostage, or he might have been angry enough with my mother to kill me." She took a deep breath to calm her heart rate. "The plan was to extract with the team, but Agus's men caught up with us and there was another helicopter coming in, so they had to leave." She gave a shuddery smile. "I was terrified, but Damien was so calm. He told me we would get away. We were lucky to find the Zodiac nearby, and he swam out in that swirling, dangerous, debris-filled water to salvage it. Agus's men noticed the boat, so I distracted them so he could secure the boat."

"How?"

"I let them see me and then ran." She shrugged. "They chased me which gave Damien enough time to get the boat and hide it."

"That was very risky," the Major said. "Those men might have shot you."

She exhaled. "I hoped Agus had told them not to hurt me. I was more valuable to him alive than dead. If I hadn't done something, they would have seen Damien and the boat, and we would have lost our escape route."

"Did they catch you?"

She nodded. "I twisted my ankle when I ran and Agus picked me up in his luxury cruiser. He took me to his house, but I escaped out the window to the ground and then Damien extracted me. We returned to the boat and then went to a nearby deserted island to contact the team and wait extraction."

"What did Agus say to you?"

"He wanted me to know what Mum had done to him. He tied me up and hit me, and I faked unconsciousness, so he left me alone long enough for me to escape."

"Why did you bring a dog with you?" the Major-General asked.

"That was my fault," she said. "When we escaped the house, the dogs chased us. Trixie——" she cleared her throat. "The dog entered the water and kept following the boat. She was hit by debris and I couldn't let her

206

drown. I used an oar to rescue her."

"Sergeant Dobson didn't stop you?"

She glared at the colonel. "He wouldn't have dared. I was feeling particularly emotional. I would have hit him with the oar if he'd tried." She didn't flinch as she lied.

"It sounds as if you've had quite a day," the Major-General said.

"Yes." It was time to get to the point. "I enabled your team to rescue the hostage before the tsunami hit, led them to the medical supplies to help Ethan, and then cleared the extraction point so they could get away. Damien rescued me, thereby ensuring you didn't need to risk any more people's lives trying to extract me and saving you time. He deserves a medal not a dishonourable discharge." She met each man's gaze in a subtle challenge.

The Major-General smiled. "You remind me of your mother. We'll take your suggestion under advisement."

Hope filled her chest.

"You may go now," the Major said.

Mila nodded and left the room.

***

Dobby stood with Jared outside the room where the corporal had taken Mila, his heart beating rapidly. Though her outrage had been magnificent, he'd worried she would say the wrong thing and make things worse.

He needn't have worried. She'd been calm, rational and persuasive, knowing exactly what to say to paint him in the best light.

And the picture she'd painted of him wasn't one he recognised, but the only thing she'd lied about was how the dog ended up on the boat.

Could he live up to the man she thought he was?

Jared poked him as Mila made her closing statement. "She's just saved your arse."

He nodded. "She's amazing." Was this proof she cared for him as much as he cared for her? Or was it simply her selfless nature and sense of injustice coming into play?

"Obviously learnt a lot from Mum and Dad about influencing people," Jared murmured back with a smile.

Dobby stepped back as the corporal led Mila out of the room. Her face flushed when she saw him there.

"Were you eavesdropping?"

"Sure was, sweetheart." He fell into step with her. "Thank you."

She nodded. "They can't possibly suggest your actions were dishonourable now." She yawned.

It was a couple of hours until dawn. He glanced at Jared. "Has Mila got somewhere to sleep?"

"Yeah, she's got a bunk in the guest area. I'll take her."

He wanted to take her himself but he wasn't familiar with that area of the ship. They reached the rec room and he stopped. "Sleep well, sweetheart. I'll see you later." He wanted to hug her, or kiss her, but if the command thought she was emotionally connected to him, it would void her argument.

He stepped into the room.

Her expression was slightly hurt, but she nodded. "Good night." She hobbled down the corridor after the corporal and her brother.

His heart ached, but he'd have time to talk about what was next for them tomorrow.

He joined his teammates who were still waiting.

"How did it go?" Axle asked.

"Mila slayed them," Dobby said, unable to keep the awe from his voice.

"I knew she would," Joker said. "The girl's got guts and grit. You're a lucky man."

Dobby didn't deny it. "Let's get some sleep."

Chapter 17

Mila was shaken awake by a female corporal who was crouched down next to her. The room she was in was tiny, with a glaring yellow light. It took her a second to remember she was safe on a naval ship. She was on the bottom bunk of three and there wasn't enough head room for her to sit. "What's wrong?"

"Your flight has been brought forward. You're leaving in ten minutes."

She blinked as she tried to figure out what that meant. "Flight where?"

"Home. Come on, we don't have a lot of time. Do you have any things?"

"Just my bag." She crawled out of her bunk and pulled on the pants she'd been given to wear. "Can I say goodbye to my brother?" And Damien.

"I don't know. I've been told to get you to the top deck. He might already be there."

Mila shoved on her military boots, grabbed her still damp bag and crutches, and followed the woman out of the door. She didn't know where she was on the boat and was panting by the time they'd gone down the first corridor.

Where was Damien?

It didn't take long until she stepped out on the deck and the humidity enveloped her like a blanket she didn't want. The sky had the glow of early morning and across the deck a man was being loaded onto a helicopter on a stretcher.

Was that Ethan?

"This way." The corporal headed towards the helicopter.

From the left, out of another door, she spotted Vance. Damn it. She didn't want to share a ride with him.

She scanned the deck for Damien or her brother but she didn't recognise any of the uniformed men.

Wouldn't she get the chance to say goodbye?

She hadn't even given Damien her number—not that she had a phone. Did her travel insurance cover natural disasters?

She reached the helicopter and was helped in by a soldier, who handed her a pair of headphones. Lying on one side was Ethan, and he was awake and wearing a headset as well.

She grinned at him. "How are you?"

"Angel!" He smiled and then grimaced. "Broken, but alive thanks to you."

She squeezed his hand. "I'm glad. Do you know where we're going? I didn't say goodbye to the team."

"They're flying us to Singapore first and then to Perth. Where are you from?"

"Sydney."

"Then I guess they'll get you on a flight to Sydney from there."

Someone tapped her on the shoulder and she turned as the solider pointed to a nearby seat. "You need to strap in."

She chose a seat across from Ethan, though it also

210

meant she was next to Vance. His smile was a little hesitant.

Good. Maybe he realised what he'd done had risked so many lives.

She ignored him as the soldier showed her how to strap in correctly and in no time the helicopter rose into the air and flew away.

She kept her eyes on the deck until it was out of sight, but didn't see Damien or Jared. Her chest squeezed as she closed her eyes.

Would she see Damien again?

She pushed away the pain and turned to Ethan. "Have you got someone waiting for you back home to pamper you?"

Sadness crossed his face. "No."

Something about the way he said it made her pause. "Have you got anyone?"

"I'll be in hospital for a long time still. Plenty of rehabilitation."

She hated the idea of him going through it all alone. "Parents?"

He shook his head.

"Partner?"

"I abandoned the only girl who ever loved me for the army," he said, regret filling his tone. "It's no life for someone you love to always worry when you go away."

Damien had mentioned that. Mila frowned. "Did Chelsea say that?"

"How do you know that name?"

"You mentioned her when you were drugged."

He grimaced. "No, she didn't."

"What did she say?"

He looked embarrassed. "I didn't give her a choice."

Mila gaped at him. "What? You loved her and you left her without telling her why?" Was that why Damien hadn't said goodbye to her?

"She was better off without me. We were both too young to know our hearts."

Well that was the biggest load of rubbish she'd heard. Was it a common misconception with military people? "How long ago?"

"Ten years. She's got her own life now."

"Married?"

He shook his head. "Not that I can see."

So he kept track of her. Mila hid a smile. "Maybe you should reconnect while you're recovering."

"Hell no. I'm not putting her through this."

He had a point. It was probably a bad time to be coming back into her life. "Then maybe when you're back on your feet."

He shook his head. "Tell me what happened after we left you on the island."

Subject closed. Topic changed.

Understood.

She exhaled and told her story again.

It was late afternoon by the time they arrived in Perth, Western Australia. Mila had avoided talking to Vance for the entire trip as she made herself Ethan's personal helper in Singapore, getting him food and drink when he needed it.

His actual nurse didn't seem to mind.

At the air force base she got his phone number and the name of the hospital they were taking him to and waved as the ambulance took him away.

The soldier responsible for them turned to her and Vance. "We've got you on a flight to Sydney from the domestic airport in three hours." He gestured to a nearby army vehicle. "We'll take you there now."

The car seemed incredibly quiet after the noise of the plane and silence stretched between her and Vance.

Mila wished she had her phone so she could scroll social media or read a book, but instead she stared out the window.

She no longer found him good looking, couldn't remember why she had. The sullen turn to his mouth wasn't intriguing, it was sulky and everything about him screamed selfish to her.

Vance had received the message and didn't speak to her.

At the airport they were given their tickets, checked in and left to their own devices.

She headed for the security point and Vance followed her. It wasn't until they were through to the waiting area that Vance spoke.

"Mila, I'm sorry."

It was surprise that made her turn to look at him. "Really?"

He ran a hand through his hair. "Of course I'm sorry. I didn't mean to get you caught up in my mess."

She gazed at him, unmoved. "I seem to recall you saying to Agus you had to marry me, which is when he stole my phone and laptop."

"Shit. Yeah, OK, I did, but I didn't think he would do something so extreme."

"What *did* you think he would do?"

He swore again. "I wasn't thinking about anything but myself. I was desperate."

"No, you were selfish and inconsiderate," she said. "You never cared for me. You used me to get a job."

He looked guilty, but said, "I cared for you."

"When's my birthday?"

He looked blank. "Your birthday?"

"Yeah. When I threw the party for your birthday, you asked when mine was."

He scowled. "I don't remember."

Because it wasn't important to him. She didn't have

the energy to care about him any longer. "It's over, Vance. I don't want to see you again."

"What will you tell your father?"

Still only worried about his own skin. "The truth. You'll need to live with the consequences of your actions, and maybe in the future you'll consider how they'll affect others."

He opened his mouth as if to argue and then closed it again. "Fine. Good luck." He walked away.

She exhaled and spotted a payphone against the wall. She hadn't called her father yet.

He would make her feel better.

She still had her bag with some cash in it, and money given to her by the soldier who'd dropped them at the airport, so she went into the nearest bookstore to get some change.

It was time to get back to her life.

***

"Gone? What do you mean she's gone?" Dobby demanded of the corporal who had arrived to give them orders the next day.

"Mila Watkins left on the flight that took Ethan and Vance to Singapore." The man shrugged. "It was a last-minute departure change. She only had time to get dressed and go."

Damn it. He hadn't told her how he felt. He hadn't even got her address or telephone number. All he knew was she lived in Sydney.

"I need to find her brother."

Joker placed a hand on his arm. "We've got a new mission. You can find her later."

He didn't want to find her later. He wanted to make sure she knew how he felt and discover whether they had a future together.

"Joker's right," Radar said. "With the exercise

cancelled, we've all got to help with the relief effort."

At least they'd been assigned to a different island from the one he'd escaped from.

"We'll help you find her afterwards," Axle promised.

He exhaled, soothed by the promise. He'd told her he wanted her to move to Perth. Surely she'd realise that meant he wanted a relationship with her.

"All right." Time to get to work.

But as soon as this mission was over, he would find the woman he loved.

***

Three weeks.

It had been three weeks since the tsunami and Mila hadn't heard from Damien. When her mother returned home, Mila asked her to find out where he was, and she'd said he was still actively deployed.

Which meant he couldn't even call.

She hated not knowing when she'd hear from him— if at all. But she'd have to get used to it if she wanted a relationship with him. Not knowing where he was would be part and parcel of it.

She stared out of the living room window of her parents' large mansion in Sydney and down at the water below. The waves crashed on the shore and the sound brought goosebumps to her skin. She was trapped, wanting to flee from the coast and not wanting to leave the safety of the cliff.

The day after she'd landed in Sydney, she'd walked along the shore with her father, but when a large wave had reached her where she walked above the tide line she'd panicked and sprinted home.

It had taken five minutes for her father to catch up with her.

That's when he'd suggested therapy.

She'd agreed, knowing she needed help. Sleep was

difficult to come by without Damien around. The memories weren't far away and closing her eyes meant the wave washed over her again and again.

The lack of sleep had made it hard to get motivated for anything except Ethan.

She called him every day while he was in hospital, encouraging him, knowing he had no one else to help him. She'd considered flying over to Perth, but it was almost Christmas and her mother would be home this year. Perhaps after Christmas she would.

When her mother arrived home from her deployment, she'd dragged Mila out shopping to replace some things she'd lost in the tsunami; clothes, phone, laptop. She'd transferred her old number to the new phone and her contacts had been backed up in the cloud so she hadn't lost them.

She just didn't have the contact details of the one person she wanted.

The only bit of good news was Vance's father had cut him off after hearing that he'd faked his kidnapping. He'd kicked Vance out of his Bondi townhouse and forced him to get a job. The last Mila had heard he was staying with a friend and was on the dole.

He deserved it.

During week three she'd slept a bit more and turned her attention towards Christmas and her future, buying presents for her family and searching for work.

She wasn't sure where she wanted to move. All she knew was she didn't want to live anywhere near the ocean.

It didn't matter that Australia wasn't known for tsunamis. She couldn't look at the ocean without her chest tightening and her heart racing.

A quick search of Perth and its surrounds showed there were plenty of jobs available, but she didn't want to move there if nothing progressed between her and

Dobby.

But Sydney wasn't for her anymore. She wanted fewer people, more calm.

Somewhere she could get her life back on track.

In the end she'd applied for everything that caught her interest, most of the jobs in the not-for-profit area. Her time on Pulau Tengah had given her purpose—she wanted to help people.

By Christmas Eve she had nothing to do. She'd wrapped the presents, applied for every job available, and she was no longer of the age where she counted down the hours until Santa came. Instead she waited in her parents' living room for them to get home from work and wondered what to do with her life.

"Why are you so glum?"

She whirled around to find Jared standing in the doorway in his army fatigues, his dark hair windswept. She glanced behind looking for Damien and then shook the thought away. She ran across the room and threw herself in his arms. "When did you get in?"

"This morning." He hugged her tightly. "How are you?"

"Fine," she said, waving her hand.

"Mum says you're not sleeping."

"When did she speak to you?"

He just smirked and waited for her to answer.

She swallowed her exasperation. "The waves are noisy."

His expression darkened, and he hugged her again. "I'm so sorry you went through that, Milly."

"Not your fault. I should have left when Damien told me to." Not that she would ever regret saving those people's lives.

"I promised him a bottle of bourbon," Jared said. "I'll have to see if I can get it delivered."

Her heart leapt, but she tried to keep her tone

neutral as she asked, "Are the team back?"

"Yeah. They shipped out with me. Good guys, all of them."

Excitement shimmered in her belly. Had Damien asked for her number? Would he call? "I, ah, wanted to thank them again. Did you get their contact details?"

Jared smiled. "Yeah, I've got them somewhere." He pulled out his phone. "Axle, Joker and Radar."

He was teasing her. He knew exactly whose number she wanted. She glared at him. "And Damien?"

"Something go on between you two on the island?" he asked.

"That's none of your business."

He sobered. "Just taking care of my little sister, who's been through a very stressful situation."

"I appreciate your concern, but I can take care of myself. Damien and I didn't have time to talk about... things before I left."

"So you want to talk to him?"

"Of course I do." God her brother was so annoying. "Do you have his number or not?"

"Yeah. I'll get it for you. I need to get a drink."

She wanted to rip his phone from his hand, but instead she followed him into the kitchen... where Damien stood dressed in army fatigues.

She blinked a couple of times. His lips curled in a smile but his hands clenched as if nervous of her reaction. He looked refreshed and clean and oh, so good.

She glanced at her brother to make sure she wasn't seeing things.

"He followed me home."

Damien's smile was a little uncertain. "Hey, sweetheart."

"Hey." She pushed past her brother telling him, "You can leave now," and then launched herself into

Damien's arms, her heart bursting.

Her brother's laugh faded as he left the room. Mila smiled at Damien. "I've missed you."

"I've missed you too."

That was all she needed to hear. She kissed him.

***

Dobby held Mila tight, not quite believing he was holding her again. It had taken all his negotiation skills and a promise to recommend Jared for special ops training to convince Jared to take him home to see Mila, and then seeing her again...

She'd lost weight. Not a lot, but her cheeks were narrower and dark shadows surrounded her eyes.

Jared had mentioned she wasn't sleeping.

She shifted to her toes and then her lips were on his and all his worries about how she would react to seeing him again faded away. She tasted the same, sweet and addictive, and he deepened the kiss, savouring her.

Her quiet moan made him hard, but this wasn't why he was here. They needed to talk. Figure out where they were going from here.

He pulled back and tucked her hair behind her ear, his hand a little shaky. "Mila, we need to talk."

She nodded. "I didn't want to leave without saying goodbye."

"You didn't get a choice."

"Mum said you were redeployed. I didn't know how to reach you."

He smiled. "That's why I strong-armed your brother into bringing me home with him." He pulled out a chair from the table and sat, pulling her onto his lap. He wasn't ready to let her go yet. "What you went through was traumatic," he said. "You might not be ready to make decisions about your future. Hell, you probably shouldn't be making drastic changes yet. But I was hoping, when you are, you might be interested in spending some of your time with me."

She smiled at him. "I've been looking for jobs in Perth."

His heart leapt. "Anything decent?"

"Yeah." She sighed. "My therapist warned me against making life-changing decisions so soon," she said. "But I knew before I left Sydney to go to Indonesia that I didn't want to live here any longer. And living so close to the coast is stressful for me now."

If only he could rewind the past and make her come with them when he'd first seen her.

"My place is about ten kilometres from the coast," he said. "Perth rarely gets earthquakes or floods or cyclones. There is the occasional bushfire, but not in the city."

She smiled at him. "That sounds nice."

"If you don't want to rush things, I have a few friends you could stay with until you find your feet." He desperately wanted her to move in with him, but they barely knew each other. It would be foolish to rush things no matter how right it felt.

She placed a hand on his cheek and her eyes drank him in. "I love you, Damien."

Oh, she floored him with her openness. His head spun. "I love you too, Mila."

She kissed him. "Then I guess I'm moving to Perth."

He grinned. "I guess you are."

Rescuing Mila was the best decision he'd ever made.

Acknowledgements

It's always a little nerve-wracking starting a new series. Will readers like my Squadron 6 team, and the more international locations? Only time will tell, but I really hope you do!

Often when I get an idea for a story, I get so excited and initially only think about how cool the concept is. It's not until I actually start researching that I'm brought back to earth and realise how horrific some things truly are.

It was like this for me when I started researching tsunamis. It seemed like an exciting idea until I watched videos about the Boxing Day and Japanese tsunamis and listened to many interviews. It was devastating and I want to acknowledge all those people who were effected by these tragedies.

I realised I needed to find a balance between reality, and an entertaining story my readers would enjoy.

One article mentioned an island in Indonesia which had no fatalities, despite having no warning system, because the people knew what to do after an earthquake. I created Pulau Tengah based on this information.

I also spent a lot of time reading books about the Australian SAS. As you can imagine there is a lot which is highly confidential so I have to thank Mick Barnes for his time and patience in answering my myriad questions about Australian special forces. I did my best to be accurate, but there were a couple of places where I stretched the accuracy–but hopefully still made it plausible. Thanks, Mick.

Coming next

Heath's story is next in the Squadron 6 series, however if you want to read Ethan's story, you'll need to be on the look out for the Restoring Lilydale series coming out this year. It might just be where Ethan reunites with his childhood sweetheart, Chelsea.

If you want to keep up with the latest, make sure you join my reader group.

https://claireboston.com/pages/reader-group